ONCE UPON A HORSE

SUZANNE JURMAIN

ONCE UPON A HORSE

A HISTORY OF HORSES—
AND HOW THEY SHAPED OUR HISTORY

Lothrop, Lee & Shepard Books

NEW YORK

FOR MY PARENTS
with love

TITLE PAGE: A soldier riding without saddle or stirrups turns to deliver a Parthian shot. This cavalry trick, which requires a horseman to ride in one direction while shooting in another, was developed in Parthia before 50 B.C.

ILLUSTRATION CREDITS BEGIN ON PAGE 172

Copyright © 1989 by Suzanne Jurmain
All rights reserved. No part of this book may be reproduced or utilized in any form or by any means, electronic or mechanical, including photocopying, recording or by any information storage and retrieval system, without permission in writing from the Publisher. Inquiries should be addressed to Lothrop, Lee & Shepard Books, a division of William Morrow & Company, Inc., 105 Madison Avenue, New York, New York 10016. Printed in the United States of America.

First Edition 1 2 3 4 5 6 7 8 9 10

Library of Congress Cataloging in Publication Data
Jurmain, Suzanne. Once upon a horse: a history of horses—and how they shaped our history/by Suzanne Jurmain.   p.   cm. Bibliography: p. Includes index. Summary: Traces the horse's origins and explores how horses have helped humans change the world over the last 6000 years. ISBN 0-688-05550-8: 1. Horses—History—Juvenile literature. [1. Horses—History.] I. Title. SF283.J87 1989 636.1'009—dc19
88-17522 CIPAC

J636.1
J

I think that if I become a horseman I shall be a man on wings.

Xenophon (c. 430 B.C.–355 B.C.)
The Cyropedia **IV**. iii.

Contents

Horses and History

Kings have made history. Queens have made history. Explorers, soldiers, artists, inventors, humanitarians, lawmakers, and lawbreakers have all changed the course of events. So have animals.

Although most people don't realize it, one of the most important characters in human history had four legs, a mane, and a tail. For centuries horses have helped to build and destroy nations. They worked magic, cured the sick, fed the hungry, and explored the earth. For six thousand years horses aided humans in changing the world. And this is the story of how they did it.

1. The Dawn Horse

Once upon a time there were no horses. In those long-ago days, the legends say, people moved from place to place on foot. They dreaded long journeys and grumbled so loudly about their aching legs that the great Apache hero, Killer-of-Enemies, decided to invent a better means of travel.

One day he picked up his tools, climbed high into the heavens, and began to construct a swift, strong animal that could carry human beings across the surface of the earth. First he made a skeleton out of cornstalks; then over these sturdy bones he spread a glistening coat of ice. Skillfully he spun a mane and tail out of raindrops, added four small rainbow hoofs, and— last of all—gave the creature eyes made from two sparkling pieces of the evening star.

When all that work was done, Killer-of-Enemies paused. For a moment he thought hard. Then the hero shouted out a single magic word that summoned up a tempest. From the far corners of the universe four great whirlwinds came. They wheeled past the galaxies, swirled twice around the earth, then, with a roar, swooped inside the animal Killer-of-Enemies had made—and, suddenly, the creature came to life. It stamped its rainbow hoofs and tossed its shining head. Then it galloped off to see the world and serve the human race.

And that, Apache storytellers say, is how the first horse was created. It's a good story, but it isn't true.

Fossils, not fables, tell the true story of how life began on this planet. By looking at the petrified remains of ancient animals, trained investigators can tell what the ancestors of modern animals looked like, how they changed, and when each species developed its present form. With the help of fossils scientists have traced the history of living creatures back through the ages, and they have discovered that the story of the horse family—and that of the human family—began in the Eocene epoch, roughly fifty million years ago.

At that time the world was very different. Great mountain ranges like the Alps and Himalayas had not yet been formed. Bridges of land joined many continents, and thick tropical forests covered the earth. The dinosaurs were dead, and mammals were just beginning to populate the world. The primitive ancestors of cats, camels, elephants, and other four-footed creatures hunted for food in the shadowy woodland glades. High overhead in the trees, tiny monkeylike animals—the distant relatives of modern men and women—scurried along the branches on their tiny handlike paws. And down on the ground in the thick green undergrowth lived another very different kind of mammal. Twentieth-century scientists call it *eohippus,* which means "dawn horse," because the fossil record shows that this ancient creature was the earliest direct ancestor of all modern horses.

Although thousands of these animals once lived in Europe and America, only a few fossilized eohippus skeletons have been found. These scanty remains, however, are enough to show that the dawn horse was a little creature, about the size of a fox or a medium-sized dog. Its eyes were large, its brain was small, and its soft teeth were much too weak for chewing grass. Although its slender legs were a little like a modern horse's limbs, eohippus had big clumsy feet that looked like paws. There were four

The skeleton of eohippus is tiny compared with that of a full-sized modern horse *(right)* or with a human being.

toes on each front foot and three on each back one, and at the tip of each toe eohippus had a tiny hoof.

The dawn horse certainly didn't look like a Derby winner, but its descendants gradually developed all the characteristics of the modern horse. As the ages passed, their bodies and brains grew bigger. Their teeth hardened and became strong enough for eating grass. And the toes on each clumsy paw eventually fused into a compact single-toed hoof. But it was a long, slow process—a process that took about *forty-seven million years.*

Most available evidence suggests that the first true horses

An artist's conception of how eohippus might have looked

were born in North America about three million years ago. They were small animals, no bigger than ponies, but in every other way they looked like modern horses. They ate grass, as modern horses do. And, like their twentieth-century descendants, they were great travelers who galloped swiftly across the plains. Some migrated over the land bridge that once connected North America and Asia. Others crossed the strip of land that joined North and South America, and eventually members of the horse family settled on every continent except Australia and Antarctica.

While eohippus's descendants were evolving into horses, the ancestors of humans and other animals were also developing their modern forms. Each species progressed at its own rate, and the pace of human development was rather slow. Three million years ago, when horses first appeared on earth, the ancestors of present-day men and women were four- to five-foot-tall, small-brained creatures who stood upright, walked on two legs, and had rather apelike faces. Wild fruits, roots, and nuts were their regular food, but they also may have eaten birds' eggs or tiny animals that they caught with their bare hands. These early hominids probably used some ordinary objects as tools. They may have thrown stones at their enemies, cracked nuts with heavy rocks, or used sticks to scoop up tasty insects; but they certainly didn't know how to light a fire, paint a picture, or make a stone-tipped spear.

As the ages slowly passed, descendants of these early hominids began to look and act a lot more like modern humans. Their bodies and brains grew larger. Their intelligence and skills increased. Bit by bit our ancestors changed, and so did the world around them.

The weather on earth was getting colder. Temperatures steadily dropped until, about two million years ago, vast sheets of ice formed in the northern hemisphere and spread over much of the planet. The Ice Age, which is sometimes called the Pleistocene epoch or the Age of Glaciers, had begun.

For roughly 1.8 million years these great ice sheets advanced and retreated across the earth's surface. Although there were some warm periods, the weather was often very cold or very wet. Living conditions were sometimes poor, but most animals survived these hardships. And toward the end of these chilly centuries, a new kind of creature appeared on earth: a smart, dangerous animal called man.

The first true humans were probably born between one hundred thousand and forty thousand years ago. Although skeletons of these ancient people show that they looked like modern men and women, the remains of early homes, tools, and art show their way of living was very different from ours. In the Ice Age people didn't know how to tame animals or plant crops. They were hunters who lived in caves or rude brush shelters and spent most of their time searching for food. They set their traps, stalked their prey, and used razor-sharp stone-tipped spears to kill mammoths, bison, reindeer, and horses— thousands of horses.

In excavations at Ice Age sites archaeologists have found traces of this ancient butchery. At one spot, near the modern French village of Solutré, investigators uncovered a three-foot-deep layer of bones that stretched over two and one-half acres. It was not a cemetery or the site of some long-forgotten battle. This vast boneyard was once a killing ground—a place where hungry prehistoric hunters slaughtered one hundred thousand horses.[1]

When Ice Age people weren't hunting animals or eating them, they sometimes painted pictures of their favorite game.

Working by the eerie flicker of a spluttering grease lamp, early artists decorated the walls of dark underground caverns with wonderfully lifelike portraits of fat prancing horses, bison, reindeer, mammoths, and small shaggy ponies with bushy tails.

Today thousands of tourists visit Lascaux, Altamira, and other European caves to marvel at these ancient masterpieces. Art critics have praised the paintings, and scholars have wondered why Ice Age artists deliberately hid their work in gloomy, inaccessible caverns. No one knows the answer, but archaeologists suspect that the pictures were originally part of a secret magic ritual intended to increase the supply of game. If this is true, it means that early hunters painted horses because

A cave painting from Lascaux. The artist lived about fourteen thousand years ago.

they wanted to kill horses. To Ice Age people, a live animal was nothing more than a future dinner.

As they tracked their game across the countryside, ancient hunters must have noticed that the weather was gradually changing. The world's climate was starting to improve; and, about eleven thousand years ago, the long Age of Glaciers finally ended.

As the weather grew warmer, water from the melting ice sheets flowed into the sea. The oceans rose, water covered the land bridges between continents, and for the first time North and South America were completely separated from the rest of the world's land mass by miles of ocean. New forests and prairies appeared in some places, while in others grasslands dried up and withered away. Animals also changed. Mammoths, giant sloths, saber-toothed cats, and many other species that had survived the hardships of the Ice Age died out. Some members of the horse family disappeared, and others had to struggle to survive.

In the New World the end of the Ice Age signaled the end of the horse's existence. Soon after 11,000 B.C., all the horses in North and South America perished—and no one knows why. Were these animals killed by disease? Were they slaughtered by hungry human hunters? Did they die because a change in climate made food scarce? Theories are plentiful, but only one fact is certain: by 9000 B.C. there were no live horses on the American continents. At the end of the Ice Age, the American horse became extinct.

At the same time, on the other side of the Atlantic Ocean, the number of horses in western Europe began to decrease. During the Ice Age huge herds grazed on the vast meadows that covered most of what is now France and Germany. But when the weather warmed up, trees began to sprout, and thick,

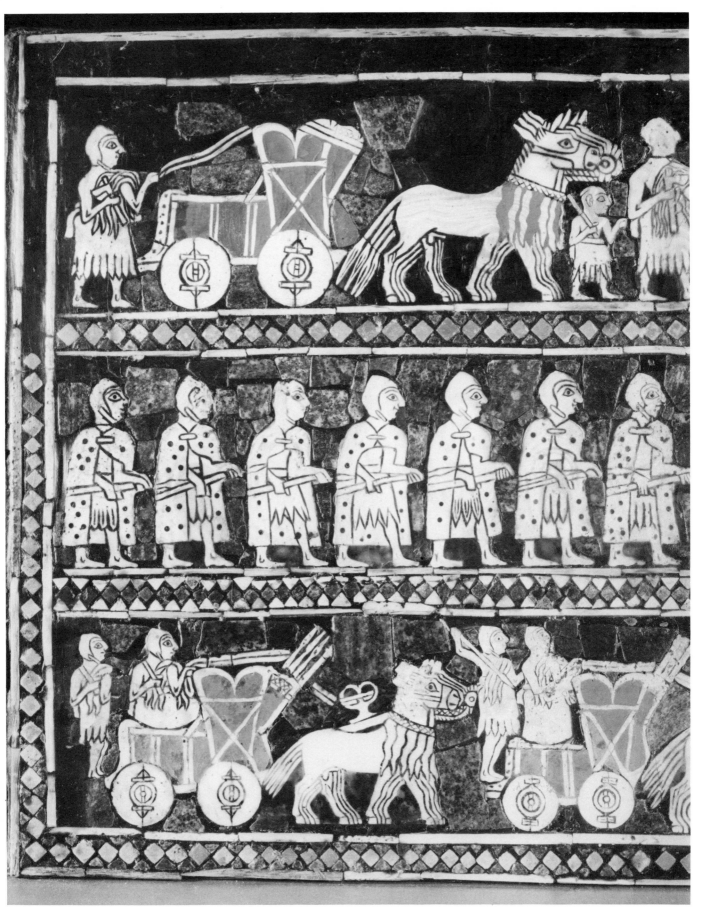

Made in about 3000 B.C., this mosaic picture shows asses drawing
Mesopotamian war chariots.

dark forests gradually spread across the European country-side. Grass became scarce, and horses had to find new pastures. Driven by their need for food, many animals left western Europe, traveled east, and eventually joined other herds of horses living on the grasslands of southern Russia and west central Asia. In this distant region the animals thrived, and by 3000 B.C. the vast Eurasian prairies were probably the horse's principal home.

When the Ice Age ended, the earth changed. The climate changed, animals changed, and so did humans. Between 11,000 and 3000 B.C. men and women invented the basic arts of civilization. They learned to plant seeds and harvest crops. They tamed dogs, pigs, sheep, goats, and cattle and began raising livestock for food. Craftspeople discovered ways to weave cloth, make pottery, and fashion metal tools. Down in the great fertile river valleys of India, Egypt, and Mesopotamia (an ancient area that included Iraq and parts of Turkey and Syria), energetic men and women built the first temples and cities. Priests drew up the first calendars. An unknown genius invented the wheel, and by 3000 B.C. people were riding in wagons and chariots.

Oxen and asses pulled the first vehicles through the streets, but travel was difficult. The big, heavy oxen moved slowly, and the stubborn, bad-tempered asses sometimes refused to move at all. Exasperated drivers shouted at their balky teams, but scolding didn't solve the problem. These ancient people needed another kind of animal to pull their carts. They needed a strong, swift, intelligent, willing steed. They needed the horse.

2. The Servant

Long ago, in the days before animals began to work for humans, a horse and a stag lived together in a lush green meadow. They nibbled the clover, rolled on the soft grass, and were quite content—until the stag became greedy. One day he drove the horse out of the meadow with a few jabs of his sharp antlers and settled down to enjoy the green grass all by himself.

The unhappy horse longed for revenge, but he couldn't think of a way to punish the stag. Finally he asked the man's advice.

"Well," said the man, stroking his beard thoughtfully, "I could easily settle the score—if you help me."

"With pleasure," cried the horse. "Just tell me what I have to do."

The man nodded. Then he went away and fetched a bridle. The horse didn't like the look of the leather bands and metal buckles, but he stood still while the man strapped on the strange contraption and let the man climb onto his back. He was pleased when the man grabbed a spear and whinnied joyfully when they set out to give the stag a good drubbing.

By evening the horse was ecstatic. The stag was licking its wounds, and the man was smiling quietly. "Tank oo for oor help," said the horse, speaking with difficulty because of the bit in his mouth. "Now, pleeth take thith harneth off me."

"Oh no," said the man. "I'm not going to do that. Yesterday I thought you were a useless animal. Today I found out what a horse can do. And from now on, I am going to make you do it."

And that, according to Aesop, the ancient Greek writer of fables, is how man first tamed the horse.

Aesop's fable, however, is only fiction. Since the horse began to serve humans long before people learned to write, the true story was probably never recorded. Today no one knows exactly when, where, or how men and women first tamed the horse, but archaeologists now think credit for this accomplishment belongs to farmers who lived on the grasslands of southern Russia and west central Asia around 4000 B.C.

At first these ancient people may have used their tame horses only for meat and milk, but that state of affairs didn't last long. Horse bones and bits of harness unearthed at Russian sites show that by about 3500 B.C. people living on the Eurasian plains had already learned that horses could help humans travel farther and faster.

They had made a great discovery. And no one outside southern Russia and west central Asia knew anything about it.

The great Eurasian grasslands were thousands of miles from other centers of civilization, and in 3500 B.C. it was hard for people in widely separated places to exchange ideas. Newspapers didn't exist. The postal service hadn't been invented, and there were no telephones, radios, or communications satellites to flash the news across continents. The first horse tamers couldn't tell the whole world about their great discovery.

And if they had, it wouldn't have made much difference.

In 3500 B.C. there were no horses in the Americas, Australia, Africa, and many parts of Europe and Asia. Most humans didn't know this fast four-legged animal existed, and it would take centuries for them to find out.

A bronze buckle in the form of a leaping horse, made about 1000 B.C. in the Caucasus region of southern Russia

As the years went by, soldiers, merchants, and immigrants left the Eurasian plains. They took horses to other lands and taught their neighbors, their customers, and sometimes their defeated enemies how to breed and train these remarkable animals. Those who learned the art of horsemanship passed the information on to others. Gradually the knowledge spread from town to town, across kingdoms and continents.

In 2500 B.C. men and women in Mesopotamian cities—a scant thousand miles from the border of southern Russia—were still hitching their wagons and chariots to oxen and asses. By 2000 B.C. Mesopotamians knew the horse existed, but it was such a rare, exotic beast they called it *anse kur ra,* which meant "the ass from foreign lands." At some time between 1800 and 1500 B.C. local rulers started to use horses for war, and from then on the *anse kur ra* was a valued member of Mesopotamian society. Doting owners gave their favorite stallions names like Foxy and Starry. Writers made up stories about horses, and princes often ended letters to other monarchs with the words "We wish you, your country, your houses, your womenfolk . . . and your horses and chariots the best of health and prosperity."[1]

Travelers like the nomads on this two-thousand-year-old Mongolian plaque carried the knowledge of horsemanship from the Eurasian plains to other parts of the ancient world.

Egyptians learned to use the horse around 1700 B.C., and soon after that merchants took horses across the Sahara and into southern Africa for the first time. Mares and stallions thrived in the green meadows just beyond the southern rim of the desert, but when travelers led their horses farther south, into the steamy woodlands of central Africa, the animals rapidly sickened and died. Ancient horse owners didn't know what caused this mysterious "horse sickness," but modern researchers have identified the culprit, a tiny blood-sucking insect called the tsetse fly.

For countless centuries these insects have swarmed

Although horses could not be used in the tsetse-fly-infested regions of central Africa, cavalrymen like this nineteenth-century lancer fought for the powerful kings who ruled the grassland regions just south of the Sahara.

through the tropical forest regions of central Africa. Like mosquitoes, they feed on the blood of other animals. When they bite, tsetses transmit germs that cause nagana, a disease that kills horses and cattle. Today there are ways to combat and cure the illness. In the past, however, there was no remedy, and for thousands of years a tiny insect and a deadly microbe kept the horse from playing an important part in the history of southern Africa.

Horses do not thrive in tropical jungles, in Arctic wastelands, or on high, rocky mountain ranges. But they can live in almost any other place—and as time went on, they did.

By 1500 B.C. Greek heroes and Indian rajahs were riding off to battle in little horse-drawn chariots. In 1300 B.C. a great Chinese king was buried alongside his favorite steeds. By 950 B.C. Israel's King Solomon could boast about the twelve thousand horses in his stables. And when Roman soldiers invaded the tiny fog-bound island of Britain in 55 B.C., they were attacked by barbarian cavalrymen in horse-drawn chariots.

Another fifteen hundred years passed before Americans discovered that horses existed. The great moment came in 1493, the year Admiral Christopher Columbus made his second voyage to the New World. Their majesties the king and queen of Spain supplied the ships, bought the provisions, and ordered twenty well-equipped lancers to accompany the expedition. But on the way to the dock the cavalrymen sold their purebred steeds and squandered most of their profits on wine, using the remainder to buy twenty cheap, broken-down nags.

By the time Columbus found out what had happened, it was too late to make amends. On September 25, 1493, the admiral, the dishonest cavalrymen, and twenty decrepit horses sailed out of Cadiz. Several weeks later the ships dropped anchor near the island of Haiti. Six of the elderly nags went ashore—and made history. They were the first horses to set foot in the New World since 9000 B.C.

Other explorers soon followed Columbus. In the next few decades European colonists shipped hundreds of horses across the Atlantic,[2] and Native Americans were startled by their first glimpse of these strange new four-legged beasts. When a Spanish soldier accidentally tumbled off his charger, Peruvians thought the whole animal had broken in two. In New Mexico Indians tried to acquire horse power by rubbing horse sweat onto their own bodies. And on March 25, 1519, a whole army of brave, experienced Mexican warriors turned tail and fled from twelve Spanish cavalrymen. The Mexicans—who'd never seen horses before—thought they were being attacked by four-legged fiends with human faces.

While some Europeans were building homes and farms in the New World, others kept on traveling. They started to explore the Pacific Ocean, and in 1601 a Portuguese navigator sighted another new continent: Australia. By 1770 Captain James Cook had claimed part of this territory for Great Britain, and in 1788 Captain Arthur Phillip brought the first British settlers and the first horses to the island continent.

The settlers—a group of convicts yanked from British jails—weren't very enthusiastic about serving their sentences on an untamed lump of land half a world away from England. The horses apparently had no objections to their new home. Soon after landing, four of Captain Phillip's six animals escaped from their groom and ran off to live in the grassy meadows along Australia's east coast. For a while Phillip and his colonists had to make do with the remaining mare and stallion, but not for long. Other ships soon brought more horses. The animals quickly multiplied, and a hundred years after Captain Phillip's ships first dropped anchor in Sydney harbor, horses

This sixteenth-century Indian drawing shows General Hernando Cortez, the Spanish conqueror of Mexico, with one of the first European horses to reach the Americas.

were pulling wagons and carriages through the streets of Australian cities. They were dragging plows across Australian farms, herding cattle on Australian ranches, and carrying explorers, doctors, policemen, and bandits across the continent.

By 1888 almost sixty centuries had passed since someone living on the vast Eurasian plains first tamed a horse. In that six-thousand-year span travelers had taken horses to every part

THE SERVANT

27

King Louis XIV's elegant stables at Versailles, about 1690

of the civilized world. Men and women on six continents had mastered the art of horsemanship. People had discovered that the horse was a valuable servant, and millions had decided that this swift, intelligent animal deserved exceptional care.

Right from the first, horses were well bred, well housed, and well fed. Pigs, sheep, and cattle lived in the open fields. Many humans lived in slums, but horses usually had more comfortable accommodations. In 1200 B.C. Anatolian horses lived in better quarters than their grooms. Twenty-eight hundred years later, little had changed. When Louis XIV built a magnificent stable at Versailles, one German prince said with a sigh, "The King of France's horses are better lodged than I."[3]

Inside these elegant horse palaces animals generally led a pleasant life. The oldest surviving book on horse care, written by a Mesopotamian trainer named Kikkuli, shows that in 1360 B.C. horses were treated like guests at a luxurious health spa. In between workouts they were bathed, massaged with butter, and fed a nourishing, high-priced diet of grass and grain.

For centuries horses ate better food than most livestock and better meals than many people. Most grooms knew horses thrived on a combination of grass and grain, but some owners seemed to feel their animals needed a more exotic diet. Legends say the Japanese hero Yokoyama Shogen always fed his mount, Onikage, minced humans. Real-life horses occasionally feasted on wine, beer, curry, and oysters. And in 1651, when most peasants lived on bread and cabbage, two French noblemen fed their horses three hundred eggs apiece before a single race.

Most tame animals are smaller than their wild relatives, but horses are larger. Over the centuries good food probably helped increase the animals' size—and so did careful breeding. Three-thousand-year-old stud books found in the ruins of Mesopotamian cities show that even in ancient times owners were trying to produce bigger, faster, stronger horses. They succeeded brilliantly, and fairly large breeds became common around 1000 B.C. As the generations passed, individual breeders continued to encourage this trend, and in A.D. 1541 England's King Henry VIII decreed that no stallion less than fifteen hands high could graze on public land.[4]

Tame horses had the best of everything: good food, good homes, good care—and one other advantage. They were seldom eaten. For the past ten thousand years humans have regularly dined on tame pigs, sheep, goats, and cattle. Ice Age hunters slaughtered and consumed wild horses. But after people tamed the horse and learned to use it, many of them stopped eating horseflesh, and some considered it a forbidden food.

Ancient Greeks and Romans refused to touch horsemeat unless they were starving. Jews, Buddhists, Moslems, and Hindus did not approve of eating it. Neither did most Christians, and in A.D. 732 Pope Gregory III ordered Catholics to avoid the dish. Some medieval European kings banned horsemeat consumption because they wanted to increase their supply of warhorses, and until 1830 it was illegal to sell horseflesh in the city of Paris.

Some of the people who made these rules honestly believed that horsemeat was unhealthy. Some thought eating it was an unholy, pagan practice. But in the past most of those who shunned the food probably did so for a simple, practical reason. They knew that a live tame horse was far more useful than a dead roasted one.

Today many of these old taboos have disappeared. In the twentieth century few people need workhorses, and many Asians, Europeans, and Americans have discovered that horsemeat makes a cheap, tasty, nourishing meal. Before 1900, however, only certain tribes living in parts of eastern Europe, central Asia, and the Americas ate horseflesh regularly—and even they were careful. Most of the meat in their cooking pots came from the carcasses of wild horses, or animals that were too old or crippled to work. Like many others these tribespeople firmly believed that a tame, healthy, well-trained horse was much too valuable to eat.

No other domestic animal has ever been so pampered and protected. No other animal has ever received such consistently good care—and no other domestic animal has ever deserved it more. For six thousand years the horse received special treatment because it was special. It was the only four-legged animal that ever changed the way humans lived, fought, worked, and played.

3. The War-Horse

Long ago, in the days when the world was new, Athena, the Greek goddess of wisdom, and Poseidon, god of the sea, held a contest to see which of them could give the greatest gift to humanity. Zeus, the mighty ruler of the gods, judged the proceedings, and all the other immortals gathered around to watch.

Athena began. She struck the ground with her shining bronze spear, and instantly the world's first olive tree sprouted from the rocky soil. Poseidon was not to be outdone. With a single blow of his trident, he split the earth wide open, and out of the murky underground caverns leaped the first horse: a splendid white stallion.

The contest was over, and Zeus rose to deliver the verdict. "You have both done well," he said. "Both are great gifts, but in days to come mortals will use one well and the other badly. They will use the horse for war and make it into an instrument of destruction. But the olive tree will give them food, oil, wood, comfort, and prosperity. The prize, therefore, belongs to Athena, and future generations will bless her for her generous gift."

This story is a myth, and like many other myths, it contains a small kernel of fact. In this case history shows that Zeus was right. Soon after people tamed the horse, they used it in battle. For thousands of years fighting was the horse's most important occupation, and in some societies it was the only important job this animal had. In Asia, the Near East, North Africa, and ancient Europe, oxen, mules, and buffaloes plowed the fields, turned machinery, and hauled freight. Horses were reserved for the dangerous, exciting business of war.

No one knows exactly when—or where—horses first marched into battle, but it seems fairly certain that the warhorse's long career began on the great plains of southern Russia and west central Asia. At some time around 2500 B.C. a group of soldiers who lived in this lonely part of the world probably decided to try an experiment. One day they climbed into little, lightweight two-wheeled chariots, drove into battle, and discovered that the horse was a military marvel.

With the help of this fast four-legged animal armies could carry out swift raids and execute complex battlefield maneuvers in double-quick time. Horses could move men and equipment across country at breakneck speed, shatter the enemy's line with a furious charge, or even help a defeated army beat a

An Assyrian war chariot in action, ninth century B.C.

Assyrian horsemen pursuing their Arab enemies, who flee on camelback. In the seventh century B.C., when this stone relief was carved, mounted archers were beginning to replace war chariots on the battlefield.

hasty retreat. Soldiers who'd never seen horses were terrified of them. And sometimes the sight of a charging war-horse with teeth bared and hoofs flying was enough to make veteran infantrymen take to their heels in panic.

The horse was a great weapon—and for a time it was also a great military secret. At first only the tribes living in and around the Eurasian plains knew how to use it in battle. And use it they did. Starting around 2000 B.C. many of these people climbed into their chariots, left their homelands, and began to use horses to conquer the world.

One by one the oldest, most powerful nations on earth fell

before bands of fierce barbarian invaders from the northern plains. Around 1700 B.C. Egypt was conquered by the chariot-driving Hyksos. Between 1800 and 1500 B.C. the great city of Babylon fell to the horse-owning Kassites. And around 1500 B.C. horses helped Aryan warriors master India.

By 1000 B.C. horse-drawn chariots were standard equipment in most armies, and soldiers had discovered that the world's greatest weapon was also the world's greatest nuisance. In the first place, the chariot was hard to use. A two-man chariot team could manage nicely if one man drove while the other bombarded the enemy with spears or arrows. But when a soldier drove alone, he had to tie the reins around his waist and control the horses with his body in order to keep his hands free for fighting. Since most chariots had no seats, the passengers and driver had to stand. They struggled to keep their balance as the little cart careened across country like a crazy roller coaster car and fought to keep their tempers when the chariot came to a sudden, unexpected halt. Such stops occurred frequently because chariots had to be carried across rivers and hoisted over hedges. They fell into ruts and wouldn't roll over rocks. They were too wide to squeeze through narrow mountain passes and so fragile that they broke down regularly.

There had to be a better way to use horses in battle, and eventually soldiers found it. Around 900 B.C. men learned to fight on horseback. Generals discovered that horsemen could outrun and outmaneuver chariots. Mounted cavalrymen began to fight the world's great battles, and in the next fourteen centuries the Huns and Mongols—two fierce tribes from the plains of central Asia—proved that hard-riding warriors could change history.

At first they didn't look like world-shakers. In the begin-

Silver Macedonian coin (460–454 B.C.) shows a mounted spearman riding without saddle or stirrups.

ning both tribes were poor wandering herders who lived in grubby felt tents and spent most of their time driving animals from pasture to pasture. They had no farms, no villages, no luxuries, and no schooling—but they did have horses.

Huge herds of wild horses raced across the central Asian plains, and the tribespeople used these animals in every imaginable way. Horsemeat was their favorite food. Mare's milk was their favorite drink, and *kumiss,* an alcoholic beverage made of fermented mare's milk, was their favorite liquor. Their leather goods were made of horsehide, and their ropes were twisted horsehair. Their clothes helped make fashion history; around 700 B.C.—when everyone else was wearing skirts, robes, and sandals—the mounted nomads who lived on the Eurasian plains put on trousers and boots, the world's first and only practical riding clothes.

Such garments were a necessity because these tribespeople practically lived on horseback. Babies took riding lessons before they could toddle. Adults thought riding was as natural as walking; and everyone worked, played, fought, gossiped, and—occasionally—ate and slept on the backs of their lean, shaggy ponies.

For many years the highly civilized Chinese looked down on their central Asian neighbors. They made fun of the barbarian horsemen and their funny clothes. But around 320 B.C. the laughing stopped.

At about that time one of these central Asian tribes—the Huns—rose to power. They swept down from the steppes, raided villages on the Chinese border, and introduced the Chinese to a new and terrifying kind of high-speed, hit-and-run cavalry warfare. The Huns wore no armor. They fought with bows, and they moved so fast that enemies never knew where or when they would strike next. Time after time the Huns attacked without warning. They swooped down on the enemy like a swarm of angry bees, vanished suddenly, and then struck again—and again—until their opponents were breathless and beaten.

Chinese armies couldn't stop the Huns, and no wonder. In 320 B.C. their cavalrymen still dressed in long, confining gowns, rode in old-fashioned chariots, and fought with short swords. Defeat followed defeat until Wu Ling, ruler of a little Chinese border state called Chao, thought of a way to give the marauding Huns a taste of their own medicine.

Between 320 and 298 B.C. Wu Ling patiently taught his Chinese soldiers to ride like Huns and shoot like Huns. But when he ordered the men to dress like Huns, his troops were outraged. None of them wanted to put on the barbarians' funny-looking breeches. Embarrassed officers begged the general to change his mind. A few considered mutiny. But the order stood—and when Wu Ling led his newly trained and trousered cavalrymen into battle, they beat the Huns and won an impressive victory.

From then on trousers had a permanent place in Chinese wardrobes, and mounted horsemen had a permanent place in Chinese armies. But the Huns kept right on attacking China, and no matter how hard they tried, Chinese cavalrymen were never quite good enough to crush the central Asian horsemen completely. Each year the tribe grew more dangerous, and in 221 B.C. Emperor Ch'in Shih Huang Ti decided it was time for drastic measures. He ordered his subjects to build a massive wall that would keep the Huns and their horses out for good.

Urged on by the sting of the overseer's lash, half a million Chinese set to work. They dug foundations, hauled stones, and laid bricks until, after about ten years, the emperor's Great Wall of China was complete. It was the greatest fortification ever built, a huge twenty-five-foot-high barrier that still stretches across fifteen hundred miles of northern Asia.

The wall has no military value now, but in 200 B.C. it may have been effective. Soon after it was built, the Huns stopped attacking China. Instead they mounted their shaggy ponies, rode west, and soon invaded Europe.

No European army could stand against them, and by A.D. 450 the Huns had conquered a mighty empire that stretched across much of what is now Russia, Poland, and Germany. But that still wasn't enough. In 452, under the leadership of their great general, Attila, the Huns invaded Italy. They helped destroy the ancient Roman Empire and might have gone on to conquer the world if an accident hadn't intervened. One night in 453 Attila, the victor of a hundred battles, suddenly died from a nosebleed. No other leader was able to take his place, and the empire began to break up. Gradually the tribesmen scattered. The Huns ceased to be a threat, and people all across Europe and Asia breathed a sigh of relief.

Then it all happened again.

Out on the plains of central Asia another tribe of wandering horsemen rose to power. They formed a mighty army, and in 1206 a ruthless chieftain called Genghis Khan led this highly disciplined troop of Mongol soldiers out to conquer the world.

Down from the steppes the Mongols came. To a contemporary chronicler they were like "devils loosed out of Hell . . . spoiling the eastern confines with fire and sword, ruining cities, cutting up woods, rooting up vineyards."[1]

They swept across Asia and conquered the greatest land empire ever known. By 1279 the Mongols governed 5,250,000 square miles of territory, and their holdings stretched from the Pacific coast of Asia to the Black Sea. A Mongol emperor, Ku-

A Mongol mobile home. Medieval European travelers reported that the nomadic Mongols lived in circular felt tents that were moved from place to place on wagons drawn by oxen.

blai Khan, sat on the Chinese throne, and people from central Asia, Persia, and Russia bowed to Mongol rulers.

No one could beat the Mongols because no one could catch them. Like the Huns, Mongol warriors specialized in swift long-distance marches, surprise attacks, and quick getaways. On campaign these cavalrymen sprinted across country at an extraordinary rate, covering as much as ninety miles in a single day. Enemies wondered how the Mongols did it. The answer was simple: good horses and nonstop travel.

Mongol horses weren't particularly fast or particularly pretty, but they were tough. These chunky, short-legged ponies needed little food, little water, and little rest. They could go for

Chinese painting of a Mongol archer and his horse

miles without stopping, and Mongol warriors knew how to get the best possible mileage out of their mounts. Since heavy loads slow horses down, a tribesman traveled light. Aside from the clothes on his back, a Mongol soldier carried only a helmet, a small pack, a leather-covered wicker shield, and his weapons: a bow, arrows, and a javelin or sword.

On campaign, troops could travel round the clock because they changed horses often. Each warrior had his own string of remounts, and on the march these well-trained animals trotted along behind their master like a pack of large, obedient dogs. As soon as one horse started to tire, the rider switched to another and hurried on.

There were no poky supply wagons to slow the pace of Genghis Khan's army. In wartime all Mongol troops lived off the land. Horses foraged for grass. Men shot game when they had a few spare moments; but if time was short, they lived on fast food supplied by horses. At breakfast a hurrying soldier often took a little dried horse milk out of his pack, mixed it with water, and gulped it down. At dinnertime he sometimes stopped just long enough to swallow a cupful of blood that he'd carefully siphoned out of his horse's veins. This warm, sticky fluid probably wasn't especially tasty, but it was nutritious, and a hungry cavalryman could extract a pint of blood every ten days without injuring his mount.

Horses were the key to Mongol military success, and the tribesmen knew it. These warriors loved their horses and gave them special attention. Although horsemeat was a popular central Asian dish, no Mongol soldier ever willingly slaughtered war-horses for food. Animals too old for battle were usually put out to pasture and left to enjoy a peaceful old age. Owners mourned the death of their favorite mounts, and hard-bitten

Mongol warriors often sang of the beauty, strength, and valor of their steeds.

In central Asia horses were plentiful, and whole armies went to war on horseback. In ancient Europe, however, horses were scarce and cavalrymen few. There well-trained legions of foot soldiers did most of the fighting until the fifth century A.D., when the Huns and other barbarian horsemen began to attack the Roman Empire. To fight these mounted invaders, Europeans developed their own special style of cavalry fighting. And around A.D. 700 a new kind of warrior began to change European history: the armored knight.

In almost every European language except English, the word for knight means "horseman." This is logical because the most important part of an armored soldier's equipment was his charger. A medieval knight couldn't walk very far in his iron shoes, and he couldn't run very fast in his clanking metal suit. In fact, the only thing that made this metal monster mobile was his horse.

Today people picture a knight's horse as an enormous beast that looked something like a cross between a Clydesdale and King Kong. But between A.D. 700 and 1300, the golden age of armored horsemen, the knight's charger was usually an active, medium-sized animal[2] that could jump a fence or gallop across a field—slowly. A racehorse with a lightweight jockey aboard has a top speed of about forty miles per hour. A medieval warhorse carrying a 150-pound man and another 100 pounds of armor, trappings, and weapons probably charged at a rate of twelve to fifteen miles per hour.

Since traveling in a heavy metal suit was difficult, knights couldn't carry out the kind of swift long-distance marches and hit-and-run raids that made central Asian warriors famous. The armored knight depended on strength, not speed. He spe-

42

cialized in cavalry charges and hand-to-hand combat and did most of his fighting in formal, well-organized battles.

On a certain day two opposing armies would camp on either side of a large field. The knights strapped on their armor and clambered up onto their high-backed wooden saddles. Squires handed each horseman a long lance, and on either side of the battlefield the mounted men formed a long line. At a signal each man put spurs to his horse and began to move forward. They went slowly at first. Then, gradually, the horses picked up speed. The men leveled their lances. The horses started to gallop—and the two opposing lines of cavalrymen rushed together like giant locomotives on a collision course. In this first furious charge each man tried to use his lance to kill, wound, or unseat his opponent. Those who survived the first crash bashed each other with swords, maces, or battle-axes until one side or the other claimed victory.

To survive one of these bloody contests, a soldier needed luck, armor, skill and—most of all—his horse. In battle an unhorsed knight was usually doomed. Pinned down by the weight of his clumsy armor, he often couldn't move fast enough to es-

Fourteenth-century knights in battle

cape being captured, crushed, or sliced to pieces by the surging swarm of horsemen around him. Even a single mishap could be fatal. During his hurried retreat from the Battle of Mohács, King Louis II of Hungary (1506–1526) accidentally fell off his horse, tumbled into a stream, and was drowned, weighted down by his own armor.

In the early Middle Ages any man who owned a horse and sword could call himself a knight, but few could afford to take advantage of the opportunity. In medieval Europe weapons and horses were so costly that even well-to-do men found it hard to pay for military equipment. In 761 a would-be knight named Isanhard had to sell a slave and all his lands in order to

A lady tries to save an unhorsed knight from drowning.

buy a horse and sword. He probably thought he'd made a good investment. And he probably had.

When a man became a knight, he moved up the social ladder. He became a nobleman who enjoyed all the privileges of high rank, and he had the opportunity to use his expensive horse and sword to make a fortune.

Since medieval kings needed cavalrymen, they paid their knights well, but not with money. These rulers were almost always short of cash, so, in exchange for military service, they gave their knights lands, farms, castles, titles, and special privileges. Knights passed some of these valuable gifts along to their children, and over the years their families grew richer and more powerful. For centuries Europe was governed by descendants of these armored horsemen. Even today many a European nobleman owes his title, wealth, and land to the fact that one of his medieval ancestors had enough money and good sense to buy himself a horse and sword.

To the soldier the war-horse was a helpful friend. To the civilian it was a powerful enemy. As mounted soldiers galloped across the continents, they left behind a ghastly trail of butchered corpses, blackened fields, and ruined cities. For many centuries ordinary men and women feared the soldier and his horse.

Fears often inspire stories, and that may be why so many old folktales tell of demoniac steeds that serve death and the powers of evil. In Czechoslovakia people once believed that the devil created horses, and there was a time when many Europeans thought Satan traveled through the world on the back of a coal-black steed. Memories of mounted Hun and Mongol soldiers may have helped convince Chinese men and women that a demon named Horse-head tortured the souls of the damned in

On the right is Kalki, the world-destroying horse described in Hindu mythology.

the afterworld. Storytellers who lived in the days when the sound of hoofbeats could signal the approach of an army made up dozens of tales about phantom steeds and headless horses that foretold the coming of death. And people who'd watched cavalrymen waste cities, villages, and mighty empires found it easy to believe that someday horses would destroy the world. In India ancient Hindu sages foresaw a day when the god Vishnu, in the form of a winged white horse named Kalki, would fly down from heaven and crush the corrupt human world with a single blow of his mighty hoof. A Christian prophet, writing a few years after Roman legions razed the city of Jerusalem in A.D. 70, had an even more frightening vision of the future. On doomsday, he said, four dreadful horsemen will gallop across the continents. The names of these riders are Conquest, War,

The Four Horsemen of the Apocalypse, in a fifteenth-century woodcut by
Albrecht Dürer

Uant le prince de
galles vist que com
batre se couenoit et
que le cardinal de
pierrefort sans riens exploitier
sen raloit. Il dist a ses gens en
les encourageant Beaulx seig-
se nous sommes vng pou contre
la puissance de noz enemys si
ne nous esbahissons mie pour ce
Car la victoire ne gist mie ou
grant nombre de peuple mais
ou dieu la veult enuoyer. Sil
aduient que la iournee soit pour
nous nous serons les plus hon-
nourez gens du monde se nous

sommes mors iay encores mon-
mon pere et de beaulx freres et
aussi vous auez de bons amys q
nous contreuengeront. Si vous
prie que vous vueilles huy ente-
dre a bien combatre. car sil plaist
a dieu et a mons saint george
vous me verrez huy treston che-
De ces parolles et de plusi aultres
belles raisons que le prince de
galles remonstra ce iour a ses
gens et sist par ses mareschaulx
remonstrer ilz surent tous re-
confortez. Delez le prince pour
le garder et conseiller estoit
messire Jehan chandos ne onc̃s

Famine, and Death. Together they are known as the Four Horsemen of the Apocalypse; and, like the cavalrymen of old, they will punish mankind "with the sword, and with hunger, and with death."[3]

Legends often reflect life, and in real life the war-horse was a killer. For centuries it was the most powerful military machine on earth. Then, toward the end of the Middle Ages, soldiers discovered a new type of strategy and a new superweapon that eventually brought the war-horse's long reign of terror to an end.

The weapon was gunpowder, which had been invented in China by sometime in the ninth century. In the 1300s the sound of cannon fire echoed across European battlefields for the first time, and in the next few centuries firearms completely changed the art of warfare in the West. Horrified knights gradually discovered that steel suits weren't bulletproof. Generals found that a few carefully launched cannonballs could wipe out a whole squadron of charging cavalry, and military experts realized that a foot soldier could aim a gun better than a man on a galloping horse.

After 1300 weapons started to change—and so did tactics. When English foot soldiers armed with simple wooden longbows defeated the finest French cavalry at the battles of Poitiers (1356) and Agincourt (1415), some Europeans were startled. They could hardly believe that infantrymen had triumphed over knights. But it was no accident.

In the centuries after Agincourt, military experts realized that most cavalry charges succeeded because foot soldiers panicked, broke ranks, and fled from the oncoming horses. The experts also noted that since the horse is a sensible animal, no rider can ever force his mount to crash headfirst into a line of men or jump into the middle of a dense crowd. When generals

LEFT: Infantry defeats cavalry: English archers rout French knights at the Battle of Poitiers, 1356.

applied this knowledge to the battlefield, they found that a company of foot soldiers armed with any kind of weapons could resist a cavalry attack if the men moved close together and formed a four-sided, immovable human barrier, technically known as an infantry square. This was an important strategic discovery, and it eventually helped make cavalry charges obsolete.[4]

As the centuries passed, guns became more powerful. Foot soldiers did more fighting, and cavalrymen did less. But armies still needed horses—for a different reason. By the time the American Civil War broke out in 1861, transportation, not combat, had become the war-horse's most important job.

Before each battle artillery horses dragged the powerful field guns into position, and after each battle ambulance horses

British infantrymen in close formation repulse a Russian cavalry attack at the Battle of Balaklava, 1854.

carried the wounded off to hospitals. In camps men waited for horses to deliver wagonloads of food, clothing, guns, and ammunition. Cavalry units made up of daring scouts and raiders dashed across country on horseback, and then fought like infantrymen—on foot.

Taxiing men and supplies from place to place wasn't a particularly glamorous job, but it was a vitally important one. Attacks sometimes failed because horses couldn't drag heavy gun carriages through the mud. Confederate troops often went hungry because the South didn't have enough horses to haul supplies to the front. And the Yankees owed one victory to General Philip Sheridan's black horse, Rienzi. On October 19, 1864, this animal raced across fifteen miles of Virginia countryside, enabling Sheridan to reach the battlefield at Cedar Creek just in time to rally his troops and save a Union army. When news of this victory reached the North, the general and his mount became famous. Poems and songs were written about their wild ride, and when Rienzi died, his body was placed in America's foremost historical museum, the Smithsonian Institution.

Rienzi became a hero, but most other army horses weren't that lucky. For the average war-horse life on the front lines was frightening, miserable, and short. During the Civil War the average cavalry horse survived only six months of active service, and statistics show that in the early part of the war both armies lost more horses and mules than men. Some of these animals died of starvation. Wounds or disease killed others. And a few, frightened by the horrible sights and sounds of war, went berserk and had to be shot.

No horse ever asked to go to war, but for many centuries these animals loyally fought man's battles. For thousands of years they helped determine the fate of nations and alter the course of history. But in the twentieth century things suddenly

2000 ARMY HORSES
WANTED!

I want to purchase immediately at the Government Stables at this station,

TWO THOUSAND ARMY HORSES!

For which I will pay the prices named below, IN CASH. Horses must pass inspection under the following regulations, to wit:

FOR HORSES

Sound in all particulars, well broken, in full flesh and good condition, from fifteen (15) to sixteen (16) hands high, from five (5) to nine [9] years old, and well adapted in every way to Cavalry purposes—price

160 DOLLARS!

FOR HORSES

Of DARK Color, sound in all particulars, strong, quick and active, well broken, square trotters in harness, in good flesh and condition, from six [6] to ten [10] years old, not less than fifteen and one half [15 1-2] hands high, weighing not less than ten hundred and fifty [1050] pounds each, and adapted to Artillery service,

170 DOLLARS!

N. B. VAN SLYKE,
CAPT. & A. Q. M.

Assistant Quartermaster's Office, Madison, Wis., March 22, 1865.

A Union Army poster. Artillery horses commanded a higher price than cavalry horses in 1865.

General Sheridan and his horse, Rienzi, portrayed on a piece of sheet music celebrating their exploit

changed. Planes, tanks, jeeps, and trucks were invented, and military men soon found that these new machines were faster, sturdier, and more efficient than the best-trained animals. After World War I most army horses were put out to pasture as cavalry units traded their livestock for tanks or cars.

A few officers, however, stubbornly refused to believe that any machine could take the place of a trusty horse. In 1937 a Polish general stated that "the horse squadron was still the arm best able to move on all terrains, to engage in regular combat . . . and to practice delaying action."[5]

Two years later his ideas were put to the test. On September 1, 1939, Adolph Hitler's German army invaded Poland. On September 3 a Polish cavalry brigade stationed near the city of Katowice found itself face to face with the advancing German troops. In this desperate situation the Poles did exactly what other cavalrymen had done for centuries: They charged—straight toward a squadron of Nazi tanks. The Germans fired and the Poles fell. None of the horsemen ever reached the enemy line, and most were killed or wounded long before they even came close to the mighty German guns.

The great age of the war-horse had ended.

4. The Traveler

American Indian storytellers who lived in the southwestern United States used to say that there was a time when the sun god had horses and men did not.

Each day, between dawn and dusk, the envious Indians watched Father Sun race across the heavens on the back of a sleek black charger. Each night the tired, footsore Indians begged for horses in their prayers. But the sun ignored these requests, and finally a brave young warrior called Naiyenezgani decided to do something about the matter. He traveled straight out to the sun's house, walked inside, and said, "Father Sun, please give me a horse for my people."

Now Father Sun had no intention of giving this pushy young fellow anything, so he said, "Horse? What horse? What makes you think I have horses here?"

But Naiyenezgani would not be put off. He sat down on the sun's doorstep and said in a loud, firm voice, "Please, Father Sun, give me a horse for my people."

The sun said nothing, so Naiyenezgani repeated his request again and again until Father Sun could stand it no more. He stuck his fingers in his ears and shouted, "All right, noisy, I'll give you a horse. Take this stallion. Leave his trappings outside your village tonight, and don't ever come back here again!"

Naiyenezgani didn't need a second invitation. He grabbed the horse's bridle and danced home with his prize.

That night he carefully piled the horse trappings outside his village. Then he fell asleep—but not for long. After only a few hours the young warrior was awakened by the sound of stamping, snorting, and neighing. He jumped up to investigate and gasped. The rope, blanket, and bridle that he had carefully placed outside the village were gone—and in their place were thousands of beautiful, prancing horses. Naiyenezgani had done his work well. And from that day on the Indians were able to race across the earth just as fast as their good friend Father Sun sped across the sky.

In bygone days, when people knew little about astronomy, American Indians weren't the only ones who thought that horses carried the sun across the heavens. Greeks, Hindus, Norsemen, Persians, Armenians, Poles, and Chinese once shared the same belief. In the past all these people seem to have assumed that the horse was the only animal fast enough to travel across the sky from east to west in a single day.

And they had a point.

At top speed—about forty-five miles per hour—the horse can outrun most other animals. Until the 1830s no other living creature or machine could provide faster transportation, and people found it easy to believe that a horse could race the wind or carry the swiftly moving sun. When the ancients thought of speed, they thought of horses, and that is probably why the word for horse in Latin, Sanskrit, and other early languages was taken from an even older term that means "to hasten."

Although archaeologists think people started to travel by horse around 3500 B.C., they still don't know whether the first horsemen rode their steeds or bumped across country in some sort of primitive horse-drawn cart or land sled. Since the bits of harness found at early sites don't provide conclusive support for either theory, investigators are in a quandary. They think that early horse tamers knew how to ride, but they know that the oldest existing pictures of riders date from about 2000 B.C., and they are quite sure that the first wheeled vehicles were built around 3000 B.C. One day new evidence may resolve this problem. Right now, however, it's safe to say that the ancients knew how to travel by horse, but few did. In early times horse travel wasn't popular. It wasn't cheap, and it certainly wasn't comfortable.

Price was the first problem. In most parts of the ancient world the horse was a luxury item. It cost more money and ate more expensive food than any other domestic animal.[1] Donkeys, oxen, and camels could live on grass, but a working horse in peak condition needed both grass and grain. And in early times grain was a scarce and precious commodity.

A bronze statuette of a warrior riding without saddle or stirrups, sixth century B.C.

Only the rich could buy horses, and only a few hardy, highly skilled athletes and soldiers could use them. Between 3500 B.C. and A.D. 400 riding was an acrobatic feat. Since saddles and stirrups hadn't been invented, everyone rode bareback—and it wasn't easy. To mount, the ancient rider had to use a block, pole-vault into position with the help of his spear, or teach his horse to kneel down. Once aboard, well-trained athletes struggled to stay on the slippery, sweaty backs of their galloping horses. Brave men discovered that bouncing up and down on the bare back of a bony horse was an excruciating experience, and in about 400 B.C. Xenophon, a famous Greek cavalry general, advised every rider to buy a comfortable horse with a soft, well-muscled back.

If riding was tough, driving wasn't much better. In ancient times the war chariot was sometimes used for travel, and this flimsy little two-wheeled cart had no seats, no roof, no baggage space, and barely enough room for two standing passengers. It was an uncomfortable, unsafe, inefficient means of

The horses pulling this Assyrian chariot wear an ancient "choke" harness.

transportation, but between 3000 B.C. and 100 B.C. this tiny, lightweight wagon was just about the only vehicle a horse could pull. That wasn't the horse's fault. The problem was the horse's harness.

The leather strap harness used by early drivers was rather like a hangman's noose. Each time the horse moved forward, the bands tightened and pressed against its windpipe. When the animal pulled hard, the pressure increased. And if the horse tried to pull a heavy load, the straps sometimes tightened so much that the unhappy creature choked.[2]

In parts of ancient Asia, the Near East, and northern Europe both girls and boys mastered the arts of riding and chariot driving. Britain's Queen Boadicea probably drove a chariot when she led her troops against a Roman army in A.D. 61. Tribeswomen who lived on the great Eurasian plains sometimes rode into battle with their men. Spartan women drove their wicker carts along the roads of ancient Greece, but most Greek and Roman women never went near a horse. In these societies people thought driving and riding were much too strenuous for females.

Horse travel was the fastest means of transportation in the ancient world—and the least popular. In those early days, the poor didn't have enough money to travel by horse. The weak didn't have the stamina. The clumsy didn't have the skill, and many women never had the chance. Those who owned horses used their expensive steeds for war, sport, or delivering important messages. For ordinary journeys almost everyone used oxen, donkeys, or their own two feet.

If someone had told an ancient Roman that horse transport had a great future, he'd probably have said, *"Absurdum!"* But he'd have been wrong, because inventors eventually found ways to make horse travel comfortable, common, convenient, and cheap.

Once again the tribes of horsemen who lived on the Eurasian grasslands took the first steps. Between 500 B.C. and A.D. 400, they invented the saddle and stirrup, two wonderful devices that allowed every rider to sit securely and comfortably on the back of a horse. With the help of this new equipment any man—young or old, athlete or amateur—could ride.

Women weren't that lucky at first. Early saddles were designed for people who rode astride, but in A.D. 400—and for almost six centuries after that—many Europeans thought a woman should never straddle a horse. Although Asian women always sat astride, many Westerners objected to the practice on the grounds that a woman's thighs were too weak for this kind of riding; that bouncing up and down in this position might damage a woman's reproductive organs; and that it was indecent for a woman to sit with one leg on either side of a horse's

A carved gem, made around A.D. 100, shows an Oriental rider using an early type of stirrup. The carving is less than an inch high.

back. Such foolish fears and false information prevented many European women from riding until medieval craftsmen invented the sidesaddle, a peculiar device that allowed a woman to sit with both legs on one side of her mount.[3] Although they were uncomfortable and unsafe, sidesaddles were commonly used from about 1300 until about 1900. And during that six-hundred-year period this strange contraption did serve one useful purpose. It helped make riding a popular, respectable activity for women.

A nineteenth-century Frenchwoman riding sidesaddle. The belt helped her to keep her seat.

Just as saddles and stirrups made riding easier, driving became less difficult when Chinese craftsmen invented the horse collar around 100 B.C. Europeans started to use it around A.D. 800 and quickly discovered that the new harness allowed horses to pull heavy vehicles with ease. A team wearing a nooselike ancient harness could haul about 1,100 pounds; with horse collars the same team could draw a 4,400- to 5,500-pound load. For the first time in history horses could use their great strength to haul a ton of freight, a lot of passengers, a heavy farm wagon, or a comfortably cushioned coach.

But there was still one problem. In A.D. 800 most people couldn't use saddles, stirrups, or horse collars because most people couldn't afford to buy or feed a horse. At that time the animal was still a luxury item. But European farmers changed that.

In the early Middle Ages they invented new planting techniques and used these methods to grow large quantities of the

The horse collar enabled draft horses to pull large, heavy wagons, as shown in this fourteenth-century manuscript illustration.

world's best horse food: oats. Soon the grain became so plentiful and cheap that owners were able to raise more horses than ever before. As the number of horses increased, the price fell, and by the 1600s plenty of ordinary, middle-class Europeans were able to buy and use these valuable animals.

In most other parts of the world middle-class people never had this opportunity. Farmers couldn't raise large oat crops in the steamy tropical swamplands of southern Asia or the arid wastelands of North Africa and the Near East. In these places horse food was always scarce, the horse population always small, and horse travel always an expensive upper-class luxury. But in the great grain-growing regions of Europe, Australia, and the Americas, where food was plentiful and horses were numerous, businessmen found a way to make horse travel available to everyone. They used horses to create the first public transportation systems.

Late in the 1600s an enterprising Frenchman named Nicholas Sauvage bought a horse and carriage and offered a ride to anyone who could pay a modest fare, thus establishing the first taxi service in Paris. Others copied his idea, and by the eighteenth century regularly scheduled horse-drawn stagecoaches packed with paying customers were shuttling between European towns as commuter trains do today. In 1819 horses pulled the first buses down the streets of Paris. Londoners began to travel on horse-drawn buses in 1829, and by 1832 New Yorkers were going to work by horsecar, a type of trolley that ran on rails and was pulled along by horses. Bus and trolley fares were low, and riders liked the fast, inexpensive service. The new public transportation systems grew quickly, and by 1857 the London General Omnibus Company had 600 buses, 6,200 horses, and one million passengers.

By 1857 almost anyone in the Western world could travel by horse—and just about everyone did. During the golden age of horse travel, from 1700 to 1900, it seemed that every man, woman, and child in Europe and North America was going somewhere by horse.

Early each morning city folk heard the noisy clip-clop of horses' hoofs as drivers brought cartloads of country-fresh fruit, meat, and vegetables to market. On the highways Clydesdales, Shires, and other large draft horses plodded steadily along, hauling three- and four-ton wagonloads of bricks, lumber, coal, cotton, pianos, and printing presses from town to

Passengers boarding a stagecoach, nineteenth-century England

town. Out in the country, where the highway stopped, pack-horses took over the job. Over rocky mountain passes, across muddy forest tracks, through the roughest, most dangerous country, these strong, sure-footed animals carried 150- to 200-pound bundles of furs, ammunition, bedding, guns, ribbons, pots, needles, and knives. For two hundred years horses supplied everything Europeans and Americans needed to get through a normal working day. And in an emergency these people knew there was only one thing to do: Get a horse!

Sick? Someone rode for the doctor, and soon the physician himself galloped up to the door. Toothache? The patient saddled

OVERLEAF: A horse-drawn bus

TILLING'S
T. TILLING
JOB-MASTERS,
CHIEF OFFICE, PECKHAM.
West End Branch, CASTLE ST, CHARING-+
WEDDING
CARRIAGES
WANDSWORTH COMMON STATION
WIMBLEDON STATION
WIMBLEDON, MERTON, TOOTING BROADWAY
THOMAS TILLING
TION

up and went to the dentist. Fire? No problem there, either.
From the mid-1800s on, every big city fire brigade kept a team
of horses in the firehouse stable. When the alarm sounded,
these well-trained animals ran out of their stalls and stood beside the engine. Firemen buckled on the harness, and in two
minutes flat, horses and men were racing out the firehouse door.

The service was so fast and efficient that at the beginning of the twentieth century many small towns refused to trade their horse-drawn engines for motorized equipment. In the 1940s some firehorses were still working; and when German planes bombed English villages during World War II, old-fashioned horsepowered fire trucks often helped put out the flames.

A mounted policeman gets his man.

Some horses saved lives, and others made life extremely unsafe. Between 1700 and 1900 men and horses were often partners in crime. Together they held up trains, robbed stagecoaches, and stole livestock. In the days before the getaway car was invented, every criminal needed a getaway horse—and every police force needed horses to hunt down the criminals. Lawmen often spent long days in the saddle tracking culprits though snowy woods, across dusty plains, and down bustling city streets. With a little luck the mounted policeman captured the mounted criminal. Then both of them had to wait for a judge to ride into town and pass sentence.

ONCE UPON A HORSE

The practice of having judges travel from town to town to preside at trials began in the Middle Ages. When Henry II became king of England in 1154, most cases were judged by local lords who frequently decided issues on the basis of their own personal whims. To ensure that the same laws were administered in the same way throughout the kingdom, Henry set up a new system. He hired his own judges, gave them authority to resolve civil and criminal cases, and ordered each one to hold court in a series of towns on a regular schedule.

The British used this efficient system for centuries, and eventually Americans copied it. Starting in 1790 lawyers and judges hitched up their buggies, saddled their horses, and began to "ride circuit" in the United States, too. Instead of meeting in an office, clients, lawyers, and judges often thrashed out knotty legal problems as they trotted down the road to the next courthouse. A trial could be delayed by a lost horseshoe, and lawyers stuffed their briefcases with halters and currycombs, as well as law books.

For several centuries entertainment, too, traveled by horse. Right up until the late 1800s, many actors, painters, musicians, circus performers, and dancing masters made their living by traveling from town to town, selling their services at every stop. Some of these wandering artists tramped along the roads on foot, some went by boat, but most traveled by horse. On horseback, in horse-drawn wagons, and in rattling stagecoaches they journeyed across endless miles of back country and brought excitement, novelty, and laughter to millions who lived far from any city.

In lonely, isolated frontier farmhouses people listened for the sound of hoofbeats and looked forward to seeing a traveler ride up to the door. Sometimes the dusty stranger turned out to be a peddler with all sorts of tempting treasures packed in his saddlebags. Sometimes it was a wandering schoolmaster ready to teach arithmetic or Latin for a fee. And sometimes it was a traveling minister with a prayer book in his pocket and a sermon on his lips.

When they reached America, clergymen found that knowing how to ride a horse was almost as important as knowing how to read the Bible. In seventeenth-century Mexico, where priests were few and settlements were far apart, Catholic missionaries spent half their lives in the saddle, visiting one tiny village after another to convert the Indians to Christianity. Later, during the 1700s and 1800s, ministers of all faiths rode over miles of highways and Indian trails to reach parishioners in remote frontier settlements. But few ever matched John Wesley's record. Between 1738 and 1791, this energetic English clergyman founded the Methodist Church, preached 40,000 sermons, made 175,000 converts, and spread his message by traveling across 250,000 miles of European and American territory—mostly by horse.

As a preacher jogged along the open roads, he might find himself traveling alongside a politician seeking votes. In 1787, when the United States Constitution was written, candidates had to get their message only to the few well-to-do male property owners who were entitled to vote. Fifty years later that was no longer the case. By 1840 more than half the nation's twenty-six states had passed laws permitting all free men to cast ballots. Other states soon followed suit, and politicians had to find a way to reach thousands of new voters. Since television and radio did not exist, nineteenth-century candidates did the next best thing: they took to the road.

Before election day every hopeful office seeker mounted a horse or climbed into a buggy and set out to look for votes. For several weeks he toured the countryside, making speeches, en-

Horses helped people travel by water. In this early nineteenth-century painting, a team tows a passenger barge along the Erie Canal.

tering debates, kissing babies, shaking hands, and trying to convince people he was the right man for the job. These important campaign trips were expensive, and candidates often needed extra funds to cover the cost. When Abraham Lincoln ran for a seat in the Illinois state legislature, his supporters gave him a generous $200 to pay for hiring a horse and traveling through the district. Lincoln took the money, made the trip, and won the election. Then Honest Abe returned $199.25 to his backers, saying, "I did not need the money. I made the canvass on my own horse."[4]

Between 1700 and 1900 roads were jammed with horse-drawn wagons, carts, carriages, cabs, and buses carrying people to school, to work, to market, to church, or to the theater. Some people went on business trips. Some visited relatives. And for the first time in history ordinary people began to travel for fun. As soon as public stagecoaches made travel affordable and convenient, lots of men and women set out to visit new places. Authors wrote the first guidebooks for these sightseeing stagecoach passengers, and by the end of the eighteenth century it was clear that horses had helped humans invent a wonderful new pastime called the vacation.

Like pleasure-seekers, pathfinders traveled by horse. "Next to God we owed our victory to the horses,"[5] said a Spanish explorer who traveled through Arizona and New Mexico in the 1500s. Other scouts agreed, and for four hundred years horses helped explorers map the North American wilderness. They helped Hernando de Soto find the Mississippi River. They took Kit Carson through the California wilderness, and in 1805 Indian horses shod with buffalo-hide moccasins carried Lewis and Clark from Montana all the way west to Oregon territory.

After helping explorers discover America, horses helped pi-

RIGHT: Daniel Boone leads pioneer families along the Wilderness Road, late 1700s.

oneers settle the continent. When farmers, fur traders, doctors, lawyers, and priests went west, horses went right along with them. Packhorses toted pots and pans over the mountains, and draft horses hauled covered wagons across the prairies. Slowly horses helped pound out America's great frontier highways: the Santa Fe Trail, the Mohawk Trail, the Oregon Trail, and the Wilderness Road.

Americans and Europeans went by horse because there was no better way to travel. On a good road a healthy saddle horse with a medium-sized rider could move along at about twenty-three miles per hour, and a coach could generally keep up an eleven-mile-an-hour speed. Day or night a traveler could always count on his horse. The animal would journey through blizzards, rainstorms, and blistering summer heat. Sometimes it even found the way when the driver was too tired or sick to

Horses were widely used as beasts of burden. This nineteenth-century print shows a packhorse carrying goods past Japan's Mt. Asama.

give directions. As a rule, the horse was a wonderful traveling companion.

There were times, however, when traveling by horse was a less than wonderful experience. Right up until the end of the nineteenth century the word "road" frequently meant a dirt track filled with ruts, stones, and holes. Carriages were often jolted to pieces when they rolled over these torture trails. Horses sometimes died while trying to pull heavy wagons through the thick roadway mud. Things were so bad that a few nineteenth-century California stagecoach drivers sang their young passengers to sleep with a lullaby that went:

> Hush a bye baby on the stage top;
> When the whip cracks your cradle will rock.
> If the wheels fly off, the cradle will fall:
> Down will come baby, cradle, and all.[6]

As the decades passed, the number of horses increased, and so did the number of problems. Although it was illegal to gallop within most cities, hurrying drivers broke the law and caused terrible accidents. Irate wagon masters found themselves stuck in traffic jams. Pedestrians slipped on the slick, manure-coated city streets. Flies swarmed, and in summertime hoofs pounded dry manure into a thick dust that settled on faces, clothing, and furniture.

Travelers were sometimes stranded because a horse was tired or sick, and draft animals were often badly treated, over-worked, and underfed. Many cab horses worked twelve hours a day, seven days a week, in all kinds of weather. Two-horse streetcar teams were sometimes forced to pull ten-ton loads uphill. Exhausted animals were often beaten till they bled, and many drivers used a harness that forced horses to keep their heads in an unnatural, uncomfortable upright position.

Concerned citizens tried to stop these abuses. In England Anna Sewell, the author of *Black Beauty,* campaigned for animals' rights and helped arouse public sympathy by describing the brutal way many horses were treated. A bus company arranged schedules so that horses actually had more time off than human employees, and members of one humane society posted signs in streetcars that read:

SPARE THE HORSE

To relieve the Horses from the
severe strain of starting the cars,
Passengers are requested to get off
or on only at street corners.[7]

Unfortunately, most of these efforts were useless. After four or five years of pulling streetcars most animals were so broken down and exhausted that they had to be sent to the slaughterhouse.

Horse travel clearly had its drawbacks, and inventors began to search for a faster, more efficient form of transportation. Some thought machines might be the answer. Others claimed a machine could never take the place of a horse. That argument was temporarily settled in 1830 when Peter Cooper, a well-known New York inventor, built the first practical American steam locomotive. Its engine was small, so small that some of the tubes were made of gun barrels, but the locomotive was strong, and Cooper named it after Tom Thumb, the tiny hero in the fairy tale.

As soon as they heard about the invention, Stockton and Stokes, the owners of one of Baltimore's leading stagecoach companies, challenged Mr. Cooper to a race: his locomotive against one of their horses. During the contest both engine and horse would have to pull a car along tracks for a certain dis-

A traffic jam in Chicago between 1900 and 1910

tance. The terms seemed fair, and Cooper confidently accepted the challenge.

On the appointed day both contestants were waiting at the starting line. On one side stood a magnificent gray horse; on the other, Peter Cooper and his tiny locomotive. At the signal they started forward. The horse was off and away in a flash, but the

The railroad did not entirely replace the horse. This photo, taken about 1905, shows a team hauling goods from a boxcar to a local market.

locomotive's little wheels moved very slowly. Gradually it gathered speed, the wheels turned faster and faster, and soon *Tom Thumb* and the horse were neck and neck. The engine was stoked and hot, but the horse was beginning to tire. Slowly the *Tom Thumb* inched forward. It started down the home stretch. The finish line was just ahead. Cooper was ready to cheer—when, suddenly, a pulley on the locomotive snapped. The *Tom Thumb* puffed to a stop. Cooper frantically tried to make repairs, but the horse was pounding down the track. It swept past the helpless engine, past the sweating Mr. Cooper, and moved steadily on to the finish. Cooper jammed the pulley back in place. The *Tom Thumb* started to puff and chug—but it was too late. The gray horse had crossed the finish line in triumph.

The horse had won, but it was clear that horses would not have many more victories. In the next few years inventors built bigger, faster, more reliable locomotives. Soon long, shining ribbons of railroad track stretched across the world, and the chugging, puffing "iron horse" replaced four-legged animals made of flesh and blood. By the end of the nineteenth century railroads were used for most long-distance travel, but people still used horses for short local trips until the automobile was invented at the beginning of the twentieth century. By 1930 there were very few horses on the streets of major cities. In the early 1980s descendants of Genghis Khan's cavalrymen were riding motorcycles across the Mongolian steppes. And today very few Europeans and Americans remember the time—less than one short century ago—when every man, woman, and child traveled by horse.

5. The Messenger

At 10 P.M. on the night of April 18, 1775, Paul Revere hastily pulled on a pair of riding boots, said goodbye to his frightened wife, and quietly left his Boston house. His business was urgent. American spies had learned that British troops planned to seize rebel colonial leaders and weapons hidden in the nearby towns of Concord and Lexington on the following morning. Someone had to warn the townsfolk, and Paul Revere had volunteered to help spread the alarm.

When darkness came, each messenger mounted a fast horse, galloped through the silent, moonlit countryside, and roused the sleepy Massachusetts citizens with the cry, "The regulars are out! The British are coming!"

Frightened colonists tumbled from their beds and grabbed their muskets. When the British redcoats marched into Concord and Lexington on April 19, armed American patriots were waiting for them. Shots were fired, blood was shed, and that day marked the beginning of the American Revolution.

On that night in 1775 the swift horses ridden by Paul Revere and his companions carried a message that changed history. It was an important moment, but it wasn't unique. By the time Paul Revere jumped into the saddle that chilly April night, messengers on horseback had already carried thousands of dispatches that altered the fates of individuals and nations.

Today no one knows exactly who sent the first message by

Paul Revere and his horse deliver their message.

horse, but it might have been Cyrus the Great, a Persian king who established the world's first postal system twenty-four hundred years ago. Contemporaries called Cyrus "King of the World" because his immense empire stretched from the western edge of India, across Persia, to the shores of the Aegean Sea. To govern this vast realm, Cyrus needed a quick, efficient messenger service that could carry information to the capital and orders to the provinces.

Since that kind of regular mail service didn't exist when Cyrus mounted the throne, the King of the World invented one. He built relay stations along the main roads, hired men, bought a lot of fast horses, and put his service into operation. Whenever Cyrus or one of his ministers wanted to send a message, a courier picked up the dispatch, mounted a horse, and rode fifteen miles to the nearest relay station. There he stopped, changed horses, and rode on to the next relay point. When one rider tired, another took his place, and the message was passed from horseman to horseman until it reached its destination.

Persian couriers traveled at all hours and rode in all kinds of weather. They could carry a letter 180 miles in a single day, and their efficiency so impressed the ancient Greek traveler Herodotus that he wrote, "Neither snow nor rain nor heat nor gloom of night stays these couriers from swift completion of their appointed rounds." No one ever described the mail carrier's duty better, and today the words Herodotus wrote more than two thousand years ago are inscribed across the facade of the U.S. General Post Office in New York City.

The Persian system worked so well that other nations copied it. Several centuries after Cyrus's death the ancient Romans—who had an even bigger empire to govern—started a horse-powered postal service of their own.

Roman roads paved with huge stone blocks stretched from Britain all the way to India. Hundreds of relay stations lined these highways, and government couriers on horseback or in little horse-drawn wagons raced from station to station. Since each courier's dispatch bag was packed with secret messages, military reports, tax statements, and other important state documents, Roman officials insisted on prompt deliveries. Speed was essential, but constant galloping over long stretches of hard road in the damp European climate damaged the horses'

A carved stone relief shows an ancient Roman postman driving his team.

The metal "sole" of a hipposandal

hoofs. To protect the feet of these valuable animals, the Romans used an early type of horseshoe called a hipposandal. This piece of footgear looked like a lace-up shoe with a metal sole. It was clumsy, ugly, and hard to use, but it did the job. Hipposandals helped keep Roman post-horses on the road, and the messages those horses carried helped keep the Roman Empire running.

By the Middle Ages post-horses were carrying letters for the Arab sultans who ruled North Africa and the Near East. In Asia Genghis Khan's successors set up an elaborate mail system that was served by ten thousand relay stations and twenty thousand horses. Mounted couriers became a common sight, and it was no wonder people in the tiny mountain kingdom of Tibet once believed that a magical flying horse carried all their prayers to heaven.

During the Middle Ages an Asian ruler could easily send a messenger across a continent, but a European king sometimes had trouble getting a business letter to the next town. After the Roman Empire fell in A.D. 476, the old imperial postal service collapsed. Roads decayed, relay stations fell into ruins, and for the next thirteen centuries there was no safe, reliable way to send a dispatch across Europe. Although kings, merchants, and townships set up a hodgepodge of messenger services, arrangements were slipshod, and none of these organizations worked very well. All too often a hurrying courier rode his exhausted horse up to the relay station, found the stables empty, and had to kidnap a farmer's horse in order to continue his journey. On the road bandits attacked postriders. No one insisted on regular schedules, so messengers delivered mail whenever they liked. Frustrated letter writers tried to encourage postriders to provide decent service by scrawling "haste, post, haste" or "ride villain, ride for your life" on the outside of their letters, but it didn't do much good.

For over a thousand years Europeans complained about the mail system, but no one really tried to fix it—until an eighteenth-century theater owner named John Palmer made an astonishing discovery. He found that it took three days for a postrider to carry a letter from London to Bath, while an actor traveling in a public stagecoach could make the same journey in a single day.

Armed with this knowledge and tremendous determination, Mr. Palmer set out to reorganize the entire English mail service. In interview after interview he told government officials that all letters should be carried in public stagecoaches that traveled on schedule. He recommended changing horses frequently and suggested that each coach carry a driver, a guard, and several passengers. Some bureaucrats said the idea was crazy. Others called it brilliant, and finally the government agreed to give Palmer's plan a try. At 8 A.M. on August 2, 1784, four prancing horses pulled the first mail coach out of London. It traveled over a hundred miles at a fast seven miles per hour and arrived in Bristol at eleven o'clock that night. The experiment was a success, and Palmer's invention soon became the wonder of the age.

Nothing on wheels was faster than the English mail coach. The first ones traveled at six to seven miles per hour. Later, when roads improved, they whizzed along at a record-breaking eleven miles per hour! Cautious souls feared this phenomenally swift pace would damage passengers' health, but mail coach travelers showed no ill effects. Most of them enjoyed flying across the countryside in the brightly painted mail carriages.

Breeding coach horses became big business, and inns like

OVERLEAF: An English mail coach picks up the mail without stopping.

the Yorkshire Grey and the Bay Horse were named after these four-legged heroes of the open road. It took only two minutes to change horses at each station. Few stops were made along the way, and to save time at pickup and delivery points the village postmaster and the coach guard tossed mailbags to each other as the coach rattled by. Occasionally, of course, mistakes occurred. In Barnet late one night the postmaster's sleepy wife accidentally tossed her husband's leather breeches to a passing coach guard instead of the leather mailbag. On the whole, however, the system was marvelously efficient, and other countries copied it.

Mail coaches were a great success in places with well-paved highways, but they weren't much use in the western part of the United States, where towns were separated by miles of wilderness and the road was often nothing more than a muddy buffalo track. Accidents, unfriendly Indians, and lack of organization slowed mail delivery to a crawl west of the Mississippi. Things were so bad, in fact, that in 1841 it took four months for news of President William Henry Harrison's death to travel from Washington, D.C., to California.

Westerners wanted faster service, and the owners of a freight company called Russell, Majors and Waddell thought they could provide it. On April 3, 1860, these businessmen started the most famous horse-powered postal system of all time: the Pony Express. It was actually an extremely well organized, superfast version of the ancient postrider system. Pony riders picked up letters in St. Joseph, Missouri, galloped approximately two thousand miles, and delivered the mail to Sacramento about eleven days later. Messengers changed horses at stations every 10 to 20 miles, and each man traveled 75 to 125 miles a day. It cost five dollars to send a letter, and each courier carried only twenty pounds of mail.

This U.S. postage stamp, issued in 1940, commemorates the eightieth anniversary of the founding of the Pony Express.

The Pony Express horses weren't thoroughbreds. They were tough, healthy little mustangs or Indian ponies. None weighed more than a thousand pounds, all had extremely hard hoofs, and most had very little training. One Pony Express station keeper claimed a horse was ready for use "when a rider could lead it out of the station without getting his head kicked off."[1]

The sixty riders who carried the mail were just as tough as their mounts. They were skinny young men about eighteen years old who promised not to swear, gamble, get drunk, or mistreat animals while employed by the company. They were paid about $100 to $125 a month and were expected to risk their lives daily.

On horseback these express riders carried the mail across the scorching Nevada wastelands and through Rocky Mountain passes, where the snow was sometimes thirty-two feet deep. In lowland swamps they were almost eaten alive by swarms of hungry mosquitoes, and on desert trails they kept a sharp lookout for rattlesnakes. Indians sometimes shot riders or attacked stations. The relay system sometimes failed, and rider William Cody (later known as Buffalo Bill) once had to travel 322 miles without stopping.

The life was hard, but the men and horses who worked for the Pony Express did earn a place in history. In November 1860 they raced across country to tell westerners that Abraham Lincoln had been elected president. Two months later Pony Express riders were on the road again. This time they carried vitally important messages that kept the western states from fighting on the side of the Confederacy during the Civil War.

But even as the Pony Express riders were galloping across the plains, the service they provided was becoming obsolete. On October 24, 1861, workmen finished laying the cable for the first transcontinental telegraph line. From that day on, messages could travel from New York to San Francisco in the space of a few seconds. No horse could race against the clicking telegraph key, and after only a year of operation, the Pony Express went out of business.

History is the story of change. New inventions continually replace old, and in the twentieth century electronic communication is the order of the day. But for thousands of years horses did what telephones, radios, and communications satellites do now. They got the message through.

6. The Workhorse

Once upon a time, back in the days of myth and magic, the Norse gods lived in the beautiful city of Asgard. Now these gods loved fighting and feasting, but they hated hard work. They never fixed anything, and that was why the walls of Asgard were in ruins when the giant came.

He arrived one morning, riding on the back of an enormous stallion. After running a shrewd eye over the tumbledown ramparts, he went up to Allfather Odin, king of the gods, and said, "I'll fix that wall for you—if you'll give me the sun, the moon, and the goddess of love for my wages."

As soon as he heard this outrageous offer, Odin went white with rage. But before he could bawl out the insolent giant, Loki the Trickster whispered, "Wait, Odin. Be smart. Tell the giant you'll pay if he rebuilds the wall in six months' time. He'll never meet the deadline. You'll never have to keep the bargain, and part of the work will be done for free."

This seemed like good advice, so Odin said, "Very well, giant, we'll pay your price—if you finish the job exactly one-half year from today."

"That's impossible!" cried the giant. Then he paused, and a crafty smile flickered around the corners of his mouth. "But I'll give it a try—if you'll let my horse help."

Odin agreed, figuring the horse couldn't do much. And that was a big mistake.

The giant's horse worked just as hard as the giant. Each morning the stallion hauled enormous loads of stone up to the ramparts. Each afternoon the giant cemented the stones into place. Each week the wall rose higher and higher. And when the deadline was only three days away, the battlements were almost complete. If the giant finished, the gods would have to pay. A worried Odin ordered Loki to find some way out of the predicament.

And Loki did. He transformed himself into a pretty mare, pranced off into the forest, and began to flirt with the giant's hardworking stallion. Soon the big horse was so madly in love that he forgot about his job. Instead of hauling stones, he ran off to play with his lady friend—and he didn't come back.

Work came to a standstill. The hours ticked by, and when the deadline came, the city walls were incomplete. The giant raged, Loki laughed, and Odin smiled quietly. After all, he thought, the business had turned out rather well. Asgard's new wall was high and strong. The repair work had been done for free, and Odin had acquired a useful piece of information. In six short months this mighty god had learned that the horse could be a strong, efficient worker.

It took centuries for mortals to make the same discovery.

During ancient times people thought the horse was a high-priced, inefficient laborer—and they were right. In those days the horse was expensive to buy and to feed. It couldn't pull a heavy load. And it couldn't work in the fields because constant contact with damp, muddy ground damaged its delicate hoofs. The ancients sensibly saved their fast, fragile, expensive horses for sport and war. And they used cheap, hardy oxen, donkeys, and water buffaloes to pull plows, turn machines, and haul heavy wagons. Horses were excused from most everyday chores until the Middle Ages.

In this sixteenth-century European painting, a farmer plows with a
two-horse team.

After learning to use the horse collar, around A.D. 800, Europeans realized that horses were strong enough to pull enormous loads. They found that little metal plates nailed to the horse's feet protected the animal's hoofs from the damp.[1] Finally they developed a way to grow large oat crops, which brought the cost of owning a horse way down. By the end of the Middle Ages Europeans had transformed the horse into a cheap, practical, popular work animal. And they were the only people on earth who'd done it. In Asia, North Africa, and the Near East, where horses were always scarce and expensive, donkeys, oxen, and water buffaloes kept right on doing the heavy work. But after the Middle Ages Europe started to run on horsepower.

Farmers were the first to benefit. In the 1300s they realized that a horse could plow a field faster than an ox, and from that moment until the beginning of the twentieth century horses were the most popular farmhands in Europe.

Year after year, in season after season, the farmer and his horse worked side by side. At six-thirty in the cold gray mornings of early spring, they were already hard at work, doing the plowing. Up and down the field they paced, back and forth, walking eleven miles each time they tilled an acre. Summertime brought the harvest. On hot August days farmers cut the grain and horses threshed it, stamping and tramping on the new-cut sheaves to separate the valuable kernels from the straw. In September farm horses carried grain to the mill and flour to market. In October it was time for winter plowing. And when winter came, the farmer and his horse fetched wood for the fire, hauled fodder to the cattle, and rested—just a little—before it was time to plow the fields again in spring.

For many years farm horses had three basic jobs: plowing, threshing, and hauling. But in the nineteenth century things changed. In 1831 an American named Cyrus McCormick invented a horse-powered reaping machine that cut wheat quickly. Other inventors followed his lead, and soon farmers were using horse-drawn mowers, cultivators, diggers, planters, reapers, and cotton pickers. Farm horses were busier than ever, and field work was done faster than ever before. In the 1700s a single man with a sickle could cut half an acre of wheat in one day. By the late 1890s a farmer equipped with a team of twenty horses and a machine called a combine could reap, thresh, and bag all the wheat grown on seventy acres in the same amount of time. With the help of the new horse-powered machines European, American, and Australian farmers were able to work less, cultivate more land, and grow more crops.

Harvesting wheat in eastern Oregon around 1900 with the help of a combine powered by thirty-six horses

Horse turning a pressing machine in a sixteenth-century olive-oil factory

The workhorse was the farmer's friend and the factory hand's partner. The ancient Greeks and Romans occasionally used old, worn-out horses to turn machinery that powered olive presses, grape presses, and grain mills. That was the first time horses worked in factories. It certainly wasn't the last. Between 1500 and 1800 European industry ran on wind power, water power, and animal power.

To keep factory machines spinning, horses had to walk on a treadmill or pace around in a circle to turn enormous cranks. Kindly foremen blindfolded the animals so they could make the circuit without getting dizzy; crueller men simply put out the horses' eyes. In factories hours were long, jobs were boring, and animals were often beaten, starved, and overworked. But even under the worst conditions horses did their jobs. For years they powered machines that churned butter, pressed cider, refined sugar, and made gunpowder. They worked in textile mills. They worked in dye factories. And in Europe's iron mills, factory horses helped process ore that mine horses helped scoop out of the earth.

From the sixteenth century on, European mining camps were covered with hoofprints. At first mine horses spent all their time aboveground, turning machines that pumped water out of the pits and hoisted buckets of ore up to the the surface. Later they worked underground, too. Starting in the 1700s thousands boarded mine elevators, traveled down the deep shafts, and spent their days hauling coal through dark, chilly subterranean caverns. Since most full-sized horses couldn't squeeze through the low-ceilinged mine tunnels, tiny Shetland ponies did most of the work and did it well. Statistics show that as soon as horses started to work underground, the output of Scottish mines increased.

Horses hauling ore in a sixteenth-century European mining camp

What could workhorses do? Almost anything. These animals hauled the bricks that built the bridges, the houses, the castles, the cathedrals, and the shops. Horses dragged the sculptor's marble from the quarries. They harvested the timber. Some even helped to excavate canals. Farmhand, factory hand, miner, and builder, the horse was the most useful animal in Europe. And when Europeans brought horses to the New World, these hardworking animals changed the way Native Americans lived and helped colonists build a brand-new nation.

In the centuries before Columbus reached the New World, most of the Indians on the Great Plains were farmers. They

lived in little villages, made pottery, and tended their crops. Sometimes they fished or hunted rabbits and deer. Huge herds of buffalo wandered across the prairie, too, but the Indians seldom killed these big shaggy animals because it was hard to track the fast-moving herds on foot.

When Europeans brought the first horses to North America in the 1500s, they had no intention of sharing these valuable animals with their Native American neighbors. Soon after arriving, Spanish settlers established laws making it a crime for an Indian to own or ride a horse. But these edicts could not be enforced. As soon as the Indians realized that horses were use-

Most Indian buffalo hunters were men, but this painting by an artist who traveled through the West in the nineteenth century shows that some women may have tackled this dangerous job.

ful, they stole animals from the settlers' corrals, rounded up strays, and started their own herds. By the 1600s tribes on the Great Plains had already begun to master the art of horsemanship. In the 1700s they found that a mounted hunter could easily keep pace with a buffalo herd, and that discovery changed their lives. At the beginning of the eighteenth century many Plains tribes stopped planting crops. They left their quiet villages and became wandering hunters who lived on buffalo meat, dressed in buffalo skins, slept in buffalo-hide tents, and followed the buffalo herds across the prairies. To survive, this new kind of Plains Indian had to kill buffalo, and to do it, he needed a horse.

But not just any horse. For buffalo hunting the Indian needed an intelligent, well-trained animal with the courage of a hero, the speed of a racer, the agility of an Olympic acrobat, and the cattle sense of a good cow pony. Only about one horse in every hundred possessed these qualifications, and that horse often had to provide meat for ten Indian families. In camp, guards kept a constant watch on these precious animals, and when danger threatened, women and children spent the night outside so each buffalo horse could sleep safely within the leather walls of a tepee.

Whenever they smelled buffalo, these Indian horses quivered with excitement. As soon as lookouts sighted a herd, the men mounted, and the hunt was on. Sometimes a band of horsemen surrounded a herd, forced the buffalo to run in a circle, and then shot the shaggy beasts as they thundered past. On other occasions each rider dashed into the milling herd, chose a single animal, and raced after it. Twisting and swerving to avoid the sharp horns of the stampeding buffalo, the horse galloped across the plain until the hunter was only a few feet from his fleeing prey. Then, while his mount maintained a steady pace, the horseman dropped the reins, lifted his bow, and shot again and again until the huge buffalo sank to its knees and rolled over dead.

At the end of the hunt four or five buffalo carcasses were usually sprawled on the grass. All too often the bodies of dying men and horses lay beside them. During hunts horses were often gored, and riders were frequently thrown or trampled. The hardworking buffalo horse provided the Plains Indians with all the necessities of life, but sometimes the price of those necessities was frighteningly high.

While Indian horses hunted buffalo, other animals hunted treasure. In the sixteenth century Spanish prospectors hurried to the Americas to search for gold and silver, and horses helped them dig these precious metals out of the earth. Like the animals in European mining camps, these horses powered hoists and pumps. They dragged heavy stones across the metal-bearing ore to crush it into powder. And in the New World horses often had one other special job: they helped extract the gold.

To carry out this operation, miners spread a muddy mixture of ground-up ore and mercury on the pavement of a large courtyard. Then they drove a herd of wild horses into this carefully prepared pen and slammed the gate. Trapped and frantic with terror, the animals charged back and forth across the pavement, looking for a way to escape. Around and around they raced, and as they beat the foot-deep mud with their hoofs, all the bits of metal in the powdered ore gradually fused with the mercury. Men stationed on the walls urged the mustangs on with whips and shouts until the exhausted animals could run no more. By then the quiet courtyard contained dirt, a valuable alloy made of gold (or silver) and mercury, and a group of mutilated horses. Running through the mud stripped all the hair and skin off the animals' lower legs, leaving them permanently crippled. Miners slaughtered the injured horses and then

A cowboy and his horse try to head off a stampede.

finished processing the ore. They washed away the dirt, shoveled the alloy into a crucible, and heated it until the mercury evaporated and only a puddle of pure molten gold (or silver) remained.

That precious metal sparkled on the fingers of fine ladies and on the sword hilts of elegant gentlemen. It filled the king of Spain's treasure chests. It made some settlers rich, and it lured others to the Americas. By the 1590s horses had helped make mining one of the first great industries in the New World.

Three centuries later thousands of hardy cow ponies helped U.S. citizens found a very different kind of business: the cattle industry. At the end of the Civil War most of the western United States was nothing but wide open spaces. There were few towns and few people, and the grasslands stretched for miles in every direction. It was great cow country, and in the 1860s settlers started using it to raise large herds of longhorn cattle.

In the early days ranchers didn't bother to build fences; they let their herds run loose. Millions of cattle roamed freely across the open range, and only the brand on its side distinguished one animal from another. If a rancher wanted to count or sell his cows, he had to catch them. And cow catching was a job for experienced cowboys and cow ponies.

Despite the name, cow ponies weren't ponies at all. They were smart, tough, dependable full-sized horses. Born and raised on the open range, these animals were broken for riding when they were four or five years old and worked with cows until they were ten or eleven. No one knew more about cattle than an experienced cow pony. A good one could find a missing cow on a dark night or stop a stampede all by itself. Cowboys were supposed to tell their horses what to do, but many a young

A roundup on a Kansas ranch, about 1900

ranch hand actually got his first lessons in cattle handling from a wise old horse.

On a ranch horses usually worked hardest at certain times of the year. In early spring they helped bring in the newborn calves for branding. Later, in the autumn, men and horses on each ranch rounded up hundreds of full-grown cows that were ready for market and drove these enormous herds from Texas to the nearest railway stations in Abilene and Dodge City, Kansas, several hundred miles away.

It was a hard, dangerous trip. Indians, rustlers, wolves, and bobcats all lurked beside the trails waiting to attack. Water was sometimes scarce, and grass was often in short sup-

ONCE UPON A HORSE

ply. The cows could be slow, stubborn, wild, or just plain mean. Keeping track of these ornery creatures was a full-time job, and during a drive cowboys were always on the move, darting up and down the long line to speed up the slowpokes, slow down the speedsters, and push wanderers back into place.

Since no cow pony could stand more than half a day at a time of this grueling work, a cowboy usually took a string of six horses with him on the drive. He used two for morning work, two for afternoons, and since there were always plenty of nighttime emergencies, he kept the best two for riding after dark.

The work was hard, but the job was important. Between the 1860s and the 1880s cowboys and cow ponies guided millions of cattle along the great western trails. They helped raise enough beef to feed a nation, and they turned the western states into a great "cattle kingdom."[2]

The United States was a big country. By the time the Civil War broke out, it was one full continent wide and half a continent long. For years dreamers had talked about building a railroad that would link the West Coast with the distant East. The government put up money for the project, and in 1863 agents from two companies broke ground for America's first transcontinental railroad. In Sacramento, California, men hired by the Central Pacific Railroad soon started to lay track that headed east. In 1865, outside Omaha, Nebraska, employees of the Union Pacific Railroad picked up their tools and began working their way west.

In order to get the job done, these companies needed horse-power. During construction twenty-five thousand horses and mules worked for the Union Pacific, and the best of all these animal laborers was a spunky cart horse named Blind Tom.

Tom went to work for the railroad in the spring of 1866

Blind Tom hauling a rail flatcar near Cozad, Nebraska, in October 1866. The picture was taken by John Carbutt, a photographer hired to record the progress of Union Pacific construction.

and soon became the most popular employee in the outfit. Day after day he hauled supplies to the track-laying crew, and in twenty-seven months this horse carried 110,000 tons of rails, helped lay about a thousand miles of track, and became a hero to the hardworking railroad men.

On May 10, 1869, the long job finally ended. At a spot near Promontory, Utah, workers laid tracks that joined the two railroads, and a crowd watched Central Pacific president Leland Stanford drive in one last railway spike made of gold. Animals usually aren't invited to ceremonies like this, but one was present that day. Standing behind the proud workers, the curious reporters, and the pompous dignitaries was Blind Tom, the workhorse who'd done more than most men to build America's first transcontinental railroad.

Tom was one of the most famous workhorses and one of the last. By the time he started working for the Union Pacific, the great age of animal power was already coming to an end. In

This photo, taken in the 1980s, shows one of the last pit ponies to work in British mines.

1769 James Watt had invented the steam engine. By 1860 a Frenchman had built the first practical gasoline engine, and in 1892 a German inventor patented the first diesel. Since each of these machines could do the work of many animals, there was less demand for the muscle power a horse could provide. In the 1800s factories started to run on steam power. Between 1930 and 1950 most European, American, and Australian farmers traded their draft animals for tractors. Miners also learned to use machines, and each year fewer horses were needed underground. In 1913 seventy thousand ponies worked in English coalpits. Sixty-five years later the number had shrunk to about two hundred. And by 1988 there were only forty-three ponies left. At Ellington Colliery in the north of England twenty-five of these animals still haul supplies to miners working three hundred feet beneath the North Sea floor. But even that arrangement may not last much longer, for when these last pit ponies retire, authorities will probably buy machines to take their place.

In mining—and every other industry—the age of the workhorse has ended. Most of the jobs are gone. But the word *horsepower*[3]—which is still used to describe the amount of work a machine can do—remains: one last relic of a time when horses were the greatest workers in the Western world.

7. The Game Player

Ancient authors say that in olden times residents of the Italian city of Sybaris taught their war-horses to dance. Whenever musicians played a certain lilting melody on their flutes, these highly educated animals swayed from side to side, rose on their hind legs, and waltzed gracefully.

Whenever the horses performed, spectators from all over Italy came to marvel, and secret agents from the neighboring city of Crotona came to spy. The spies began to scheme, and finally the city of Crotona declared war on Sybaris.

On the day of battle the two armies faced each other in the field. On one side mounted Sybarite cavalrymen gripped their spears. On the other a band of Crotonian musicians picked up their flutes.

The Sybarite cavalry charged. The Crotonian musicians began to play. And right in the middle of the battlefield, the Sybarite horses began to dance. Twirling and swaying, dipping and gliding, they waltzed joyously across the field while Crotonian foot soldiers crushed the stunned Sybarite army.

Did this really happen?

Historians doubt it. Although versions of this story have been told in Greece, Italy, and China for two thousand years, there is not one shred of evidence to show that dancing horses ever caused a military disaster in Sybaris—or anywhere else. The ancient storytellers who made up the fable probably wanted to teach audiences that work and play don't mix. But that particular rule doesn't apply to every situation. Many games and tricks had a practical origin, and history shows that humans and horses have successfully mixed business and pleasure for generations.

Some equestrian sports trained riders for serious work. Others transformed serious tasks into entertainment. Hunting did both, which may be why it was popular for so many centuries.

No one knows exactly when humans discovered that chasing game with fast horses was fun, but records do show that by 1390 B.C. Egyptian pharaoh Amenhotep III was spending most of his spare time in a hunting chariot. On one expedition he managed to kill fifty-six head of wild cattle in twelve hours. Then, says an ancient inscription, "His Majesty waited four days to give spirit to his horses . . . mounted again,"[1] and—with the help of his well-rested steeds—bagged another forty head.

Other ancient hunters shared Amenhotep's enthusiasm. For centuries chariot hunting was a popular upper-class sport.

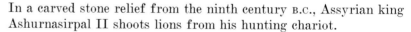

In a carved stone relief from the ninth century B.C., Assyrian king Ashurnasirpal II shoots lions from his hunting chariot.

But around 640 B.C., sportsmen found it was easier to chase game on the back of a horse. In ancient Asia, North Africa, and the Near East, riders galloped after lions, ostriches, antelopes, wild horses, and elephants. Two thousand years later lords and ladies on horseback hunted deer, wolves, and boars in the forests of medieval Europe. In the 1500s England's stout King Henry VIII often wore out three or four horses a day chasing game.

By the late 1600s, however, it was becoming harder and harder for European hunters to enjoy their favorite sport. Farms and villages were taking the place of great forests. High wooden fences built by farmers crisscrossed the old open meadows, and big game animals gradually disappeared. Some people stopped hunting on horseback, but others found a new way to keep the sport alive. In England enthusiasts started to breed horses that could jump fences. Hunters began to chase foxes instead of deer, and by the eighteenth century fox hunting had become a popular English pastime.

Ever since the days of Amenhotep, some people have loved hunting and others have loathed it. Generations of farmers complained about careless hunters who ruined crops by galloping across fields. Modern scientists dislike the sport because some species of animals have been hunted to extinction, and S.P.C.A. members correctly point out that horses are sometimes seriously injured during cross-country chases.

Hunters know these facts are true, but they also know that few things compare to the excitement of matching wits with a wild animal or the thrill of racing after hounds on a crisp, clear morning. For many the chase is more important than the kill, and some twentieth-century fox hunters prefer following a scent trail made by a human pulling a drag (a bag filled with pungent aniseed) to pursuing a wild animal across country.

Fifteenth-century European hunters chasing a deer

In addition to being fun, chasing wild game was often a very practical pastime. Medieval kings brought home enough game to feed their hungry courtiers, and for centuries sportsmen knew that the entertaining business of hunting was excellent preparation for the serious business of war.

Hunting on horseback was a lot like fighting on horseback, and plenty of good generals took advantage of the similarity. In the sixth century B.C. Cyrus the Great managed to sneak a whole Persian army into Armenia by pretending his heavily armed cavalrymen were part of a large hunting expedition. Seventeen hundred years later Genghis Khan's young horsemen got their first combat training on the hunting field. They had to. Mongol laws stated that every warrior had to know "how hunters must approach the game, how they must keep in order, and how they must encircle the game."[2] As long as wars were fought with cavalry, hunting was a useful training exercise. In the late 1600s and early 1700s Chinese emperor K'ang-hsi was still ordering his men to hold two hunts a year, "one in the spring by the river to give the people practice with boats, and one in the autumn . . . to give practice at mounted archery."[3]

Some cavalrymen got their basic training on the hunting field. Others perfected their horsemanship by playing polo. This fast, exciting game of hockey on horseback is one of the world's oldest sports. It was probably invented by Persian riders around 500 B.C., and from the Near East the sport spread to every part of Asia. Few Europeans knew polo existed until British officers stationed in India learned the game during the 1800s. They eventually introduced the sport to other Westerners, and today polo is played in Asia, Europe, Australia, South Africa, and the Americas.

Polo is an ancient game and an extremely demanding one. It requires fast thinking, good teamwork, and plenty of nerve. To succeed, a rider must have the strength to swing a long mallet, the skill to hit the wooden ball accurately, and the ability to control a horse and carry out a play simultaneously. Although some Persian women played the game in A.D. 600 and a number of Western women play today, polo has never been a particularly popular women's sport. Traditionally the game is played by men—men wealthy enough to own and train a string of polo ponies.

As a rule, these "polo ponies" aren't ponies at all. Although some riders think smaller animals are best suited to the sport, almost any kind of horse with speed, courage, agility, and stamina can play. Training generally takes a year, and at the end of that time a well-schooled pony can run like a racer, turn like a ballerina, stop dead in the middle of a gallop, and endure the punishing pace of a match. In polo a rider can easily play an entire forty-five- to sixty-minute game, but most horses are exhausted after two brief seven-and-one-half-minute play periods, and riders usually switch ponies several times during a match.

In the past twenty-five hundred years most polo players have played for fun, but one medieval general used the sport for a serious purpose. In the year 1147 a vast army of Christian knights who called themselves Crusaders left Europe and set out for the Middle East. They planned to free Jerusalem from the rule of Moslem princes. But the Moslem princes who governed the area around this holy city had other ideas. As the Crusaders marched, these Arab commanders prepared for battle. At military camps all over what is now Israel and Jordan, soldiers practiced marching, archery, and cavalry maneuvers. At the stronghold of Syrian general Nur ad-Din, troops engaged in a very different kind of training program. Each night, by the light of hundreds of flickering torches, the general and his cavalrymen played polo. If anyone asked why, Nur ad-Din replied, "We must be ready at any time to take arms . . . [and] this game of ball is the best practice for our horses, hardening

A Chinese polo match, painted in 1635

An illustration from a fifteenth-century treatise on tournaments shows two knights in competition. By the time this book was written, knights were starting to lose their importance on the battlefield, and the tournament was degenerating into a purposeless game.

them and making them . . . fit . . . and obedient to the rider."[4]

The general knew what he was talking about. When war came, Nur ad-Din's troops displayed tremendous skill and stamina. However, so did the Crusaders. Before coming to the Holy Land, these armored men and horses had improved their physical fitness by taking part in another kind of game: a type of mock battle called a tournament.

Legends say that Henry I, a tenth-century German king, invented the game because he needed a quick, entertaining way to teach his lazy noblemen to fight on horseback. Some scholars believe tournaments originated in ancient Rome. Others claim the game began in medieval France. In this muddle of information exactly one fact is clear: from the 900s to the 1600s the tournament was Europe's most popular sport. For seven centuries great lords hosted these meets, townsmen and farmers watched the action, and fighting men from all over the European continent regularly tried their luck.

A tournament was every knight's idea of a working vacation. There was fighting all day and feasting at night. Participants had a chance to see old friends and impress important patrons. Victors carried home saddlebags full of rich prizes, but winning those rewards wasn't easy. In tournament competition knights wore real armor, fought with real weapons, and used real battlefield tactics. Meets began with jousting contests in which pairs of mounted knights armed with long lances met in single combat; and they ended with the *mêlée,* a free-for-all make-believe battle fought by two opposing teams of knights.

During the games contestants were supposed to disarm, unhorse, or capture their opponents, but sometimes the excited knights forgot they were playing and began to fight in earnest. Bloodshed was common, deaths were frequent, and at one German tournament sixty men died of wounds inflicted by blunt weapons.

Since medieval knights had to protect their expensive warhorses, animals actually had a better chance of surviving these murderous contests than men. At tournaments there was no penalty for killing or injuring a human opponent, but rules drawn up in the 1400s clearly stated that "he who strykth an Horse schal have noo prize."[5]

Churchmen, horrified by all this needless violence, tried to ban the sport. In sermon after sermon priests warned that any man killed in a tournament would be sentenced to eternal damnation. But it was a waste of breath. Threats of hellfire didn't keep soldiers away from the tournament field, but changes in weapons and battle tactics eventually did. After gunpowder was invented, the armored knight became obsolete. Jousting had no place on the modern battlefield. Tournaments no longer served any practical purpose, and interest in them gradually dwindled.

All kinds of sports were once used to prepare the cavalry for war, and acrobatic training was sometimes part of a war-horse's education. According to an army manual written about 300 B.C., the Indian emperor Chandragupta I expected every horse in his cavalry to "jump like a frog," "leap like a cuckoo," do a special kind of hop before attacking an elephant, and trot four different ways.[6] Was this fancy footwork necessary? Some ancient Indian generals must have thought so, and a number of European riding masters who lived about eighteen hundred

In a scene at a seventeenth-century riding school, a horse and rider are taught to perform a jump known as the courbette.

Caprioles à Gauche

A horse learning to perform a capriole, in an illustration from an eighteenth-century book on horsemanship

years later would have agreed. Starting in the sixteenth century these equestrian experts began to teach war-horses a series of elaborate tricks that were supposed to be useful on the battlefield. At elegant riding academies would-be chargers mastered tricks like the pesade (a rearing movement designed to protect the rider from bullets), the half-pirouette (a quick turn meant to clear away a crowd of enemy soldiers), and the piaffe (a high-stepping, in-place trot that presumably helped the horse mark time while its rider bashed his enemies with a sword). All horse pupils were taught to move with perfect form, and advanced students practiced difficult steps like the capriole. This jump—which was supposed to frighten infantrymen—required the horse to tuck its front legs in, stick its back legs out, and rise without moving forward.

All this training was supposed to serve a practical purpose, and in some ways it probably did. During these long lessons horses became very obedient and their riders became very skillful. Both accomplishments must have been useful on the battlefield. Perhaps the dance steps were helpful, too, but it doesn't

OVERLEAF: Clinging to the side of his horse, an American Indian warrior prepares to throw a spear.

seem likely. It's hard to believe that a capriole would frighten experienced infantrymen or that even the best-trained horse would remember all these complex tricks in the midst of combat. Sixteenth-century English writer Thomas Blunderville thought that the battlefield was no place for a horse that "falls a-hopping and dancing up and down,"[7] and by the eighteenth century a lot of military experts agreed with him.

From that time on cavalrymen spent less time teaching their horses to prance and more time practicing rough and ready cross-country riding. But the old acrobatic feats weren't forgotten. Sportsmen came to view these jumps and turns (known as haut école or high school movements) as an ultimate test of a rider's ability to train and manage a horse. Showmen began to teach the steps to their own animals, and by the 1830s dancing horses were performing many of the old cavalry exercises in French circuses.

While war-horses learned to jump and prance, cavalrymen learned to do tricks on horseback. Stunt riding was useful on the battlefield, and almost every expert mounted soldier mastered a few basic feats. He learned to ride without reins in order to free his hands for fighting, to leap on and off a galloping horse in order to mount and dismount quickly in battle, and perhaps even to switch horses by jumping from the back of one moving animal to the back of another. Russia's Cossack cavalrymen could also pick up wounded comrades without dismounting. An eighteenth-century English soldier was taught to slip sideways in the saddle so the horse's body would shield him from bullets. And nineteenth-century American Indians learned to shoot while clinging to the side of a galloping horse. This was a particularly useful trick because it allowed the rider to fight, travel, and take cover at the same time.

On the battlefield these feats were often the key to success

Andrew Ducrow, one of the greatest English circus riders, performing at Astley's amphitheatre in 1825

and survival. Off the battlefield they were fun. In their spare time cavalrymen improved the stunts, invented others, and showed off their skill. Professional acrobats often borrowed the tricks and used them to entertain audiences. But it took an eighteenth-century English cavalryman to turn these old soldier's tricks into a dazzling new kind of entertainment.

Sergeant-Major Philip Astley (1742–1814) started his career as a soldier in His Majesty's Royal Regiment of the Fifteenth Dragoons. By age nineteen he was already famous for his daring feats of horsemanship on the battlefield. But at twenty-six the handsome six-footer had tired of military life. He left the army, opened a riding school in an old London lumberyard, and began to teach vaulting, saber fighting, and other cavalry maneuvers.

Few pupils signed up, so to attract others, Astley began to give exhibitions of trick riding. These shows were an instant success. Audiences clapped when Astley did somersaults and handstands on horseback. They gasped when he rode around the ring with his right foot on the back of one horse and his left on the back of another. And when the two horses jumped over a pole—with the ex-cavalryman still standing upright on their backs—the crowd went wild. After a time Astley decided to add a little variety to the act. He hired musicians, clowns, jugglers, tightrope walkers, performing dogs—and invented the modern circus.

On the other side of the Atlantic American cowboys found their own way to turn work into entertainment. In the late 1800s they transformed ordinary ranch skills into an exciting new sport called the rodeo.

As with most of the important events in horse history, there's a good deal of argument about where and when the first real rodeo took place. It might have been in Colorado, Wyoming, Montana, Texas, or any other part of the cattle kingdom. The date could have been 1865, 1869, 1882, or somewhere in between. Although evidence is scanty, it's probably safe to say that the first rodeos were pretty casual affairs. Cowboys with a day off and nothing to do got together and held contests to see which of them was best at riding, roping, and other ranch jobs. Since everyone enjoyed the games, more contests were organized. Ranch owners and shopkeepers offered prizes to the winners. Crowds from neighboring towns and ranches came out to watch, and by 1888 the sport was so popular that the organizers of one Denver rodeo were able to sell tickets to the show.

Today, more than a century later, ticket-selling rodeo organizers are still packing audiences in. Hundreds of these contests are held every year in the United States, Australia, and Canada, and plenty of cowboys now spend most of their time on the "suicide circuit"—traveling from rodeo to rodeo, risking life and limb in every event so they can compete for big cash prizes.

In 1888 there wasn't much difference between rodeo riding and ranch work, but that's no longer true. On a modern cattle ranch cowhands depend on jeeps and helicopters, and most old-fashioned western riding is now done in the rodeo ring. Out there, under the bright, hot lights, the men and women who compete in the calf-roping, bronco-busting, and cutting-horse contests are showing off skills that horse tamers and cattle herders have used for generations. At the rodeo yesterday's work has become today's entertainment.

And in the modern world entertainment has become the horse's most important work. Nowadays machines do the chores, but horses still help people have fun. Men and women still love the games horses play, and millions still think Britain's Lord Palmerston (1784–1865) had the right idea when he said, "The best thing for the inside of a man is the outside of a horse."

8. The Racehorse

Long ago, in the days when the world was new, three men went off into the wilderness to hunt for game. While hiking across the countryside, they spied three horses galloping through the grass. "My! What beautiful animals they are!" exclaimed the first man. "See how fast they run!" cried the second. "Let's catch and tame them," suggested the third. And that is exactly what they did.

As soon as the horses were gentle enough to ride, the hunters set out for home. But the trip was long, their provisions were scant, and after a few days their food supply was completely exhausted. The hungry men knew they would have to eat one of the horses.

But which?

No one wanted to part with his steed, and everyone wanted dinner. Finally they decided to hold a race and eat the animal that came in last.

But that didn't solve the problem. All the horses were equally swift, and to break the tie, the men raced—again and again. The more they raced, the better they liked it. The new sport was so much fun that none of them wanted to stop. None of them wanted to spoil the game by killing a horse—but all of them were famished.

For a while they sat, perplexed and desperate. Then one of them spied a gazelle. He picked up his bow, brought the animal down with a single shot, and soon all three companions were happily feasting on antelope meat.

One short week later the travelers brought their horses home. And from that day until the very end of their lives these three men rose early each morning, rushed through their chores, and spent every spare moment at the best of all possible games: horse racing.

Arab storytellers say that racing began in this way. Historians don't know exactly when, where, or why the first horse race was held, but they do know people have been crazy about the sport for as long as anyone can remember. In 1730 B.C. Mesopotamian king Samsi-adad ordered his son to send racing chariots to the city of Assur for the New Year's festival. A Greek myth dating from about 1500 B.C. tells of a hero named Pelops who had to win a chariot race to win a bride. Three thousand years ago Egyptian princes were holding chariot races on the banks of the Nile. The first good records of organized public racing date from 684 B.C., the year chariot races were included in the Olympic Games for the first time.

A painting on the edge of a cup from the sixth century B.C. shows a Greek charioteer racing his four-horse team.

A painting of two jockeys, on the side of a Greek vase. A victorious athlete won this jar filled with oil in the fifth century B.C.

In ancient Greece these games were part of a great religious festival dedicated to Zeus, the king of the gods. Every four years first-rate athletes from all over the country gathered in the hot, pine-shaded town of Olympia to pray, sacrifice, and test their skill at boxing, wrestling, running, javelin throwing, and chariot racing. At first only chariots drawn by four-horse teams were allowed to enter the Olympic Games, but races for two-horse teams were added later, and horseback riders began to compete in 644 B.C.

At Olympia chariot races were always the main attraction. Before each contest crowds gathered around the large oval racetrack with a set of tall pillars at either end. As the spectators watched, drivers guided their little two-wheeled chariots up to the starting line, fixed their eyes on a nearby altar, and waited tensely. When all the contestants were in place, an attendant pressed a lever, and a glittering bronze eagle mounted on the altar soared into the air. With a shout the drivers urged their horses forward—and the race was on.

Down the course they sped, chariots tipping dangerously as drivers whipped around the pillars and galloped out onto the straightaway. Around and around the track they thundered. There was no finish line; as soon as a driver completed the required number of laps, he pulled his sweating horses to a stop in front of the judges and waited for the verdict.

"The breeding of chariot horses is the noblest, grandest profession in the world,"[1] said the Greek poet Simonides. Certainly it was a flourishing business in ancient Greece. From the lush northern pastures of Thessaly to the olive-ringed southern city of Sparta, stable owners tried to produce large, spirited, high-stepping racers. Good horses commanded high prices, and talented animals were praised, honored, and sometimes buried alongside their owners in the family tomb.

The bravest, richest, most powerful men in Greece owned and drove the teams that vied for prizes on the track. The awards—usually a jar of oil for the owner and a woollen headband for the driver—weren't very valuable, but the contestants didn't care. They raced to have fun and thrills, to honor the immortal gods, and most of all to win renown. Olympic champions, the sports heroes of the ancient world, were honored throughout the whole of Greece. In pottery shops famous painters decorated pitchers, cups, and wine bowls with exquisite pictures of the winning athletes. Sculptors carved statues of the victors, and poets praised the competitors in verse.

But only men could share the fun, the excitement, and the glory. Few Greek girls knew how to ride a horse or drive a chariot. Women weren't even allowed to watch the Olympic Games, and any female caught sneaking past the gatekeepers was instantly executed. It wasn't easy to overcome these obstacles, but one woman did. In 386 B.C. she entered her very own specially bred team at Olympia and carried off the prize. She couldn't set foot on the track. She couldn't watch her horses win, but she did the next best thing. Close beside the Olympic track, this determined woman set up a statue of herself. On the pedestal she had a sculptor carve these few proud words: "My father and brothers were kings of Sparta. I, Cynisca, conquering with a chariot of fleet-footed steeds, set up this statue. And

A Roman charioteer with the reins wrapped tightly around his waist prepares to round a turn during a race, in this terra cotta relief from the first century A.D. The infield of a Roman racetrack was usually decorated with columns, like those at the right, and statues of the gods.

I say I am the only woman in all Greece that ever won this crown."[2]

In ancient Greece racing was often part of a religious rite. In Rome it was usually pure, undisguised entertainment. On sixty-four days each year thousands of excited Roman sports fans crowded into enormous stadiums to watch the horses run. Admission was free, and the show was spectacular. From their hard stone seats, audiences usually watched twelve to twenty-four events in a single afternoon. There were races on horseback, exhibitions of trick riding, and—finally—the attraction everyone was waiting for: the chariot races. Gamblers in the stands staked fortunes on the outcome of a single contest. Fans knew the names of their favorite horses and drivers, and the crowd roared each time a popular team trotted onto the track.

Roman chariot teams were made up of two, four, eight, or even ten horses. For the occasion each horse was decked in a shining breastplate. Colored ribbons dangled from its harness, and sometimes a few strands of pearls were carefully braided into the animal's mane. The drivers, standing straight and tall in their chariots, looked just as elegant in their polished helmets, leggings, and short tunics of red, blue, green, or white. The chariot reins were knotted securely around each man's waist, and at his side every driver carried a sharp knife to cut the traces in case of accident.

Up in the official box, the presiding consul dressed in robes of purple and scarlet rose from his seat, stretched out his hand, and dropped a white handkerchief into the arena. Trumpets blared. The drivers cracked their whips, and the horses bolted forward in a cloud of dust.

Seven times the chariots circled the track, a total distance of about five miles. Drivers deliberately bumped and jostled

Roman emperor
Maximian drives a
four-horse triumphal
chariot (quadriga) on a
gold coin minted in A.D.
297.

each other. From time to time the rattle of wheels and the
steady drumming of hoofs was punctuated by the crash of col-
liding chariots or a scream as a car overturned, spilling driver
and horses right into the path of the oncoming teams. At the
end there were cheers, a branch of palm, or a golden wreath for
the winner. Losers were often carried off on stretchers to the
doctor or the morgue.

Almost every Roman, from the smallest schoolboy to the
mighty, all-powerful emperor, secretly dreamed of becoming a
great charioteer.[3] But the men who actually risked their lives
on the track were usually low-born commoners or slaves. Those
who survived long enough to win an impressive number of victories also won fame, freedom, and enough cash to enable them
to retire as wealthy men.

Roman charioteers became heroes—and so did their horses.
Racegoers in every corner of the empire knew the names, pedi-
grees, characteristics, and records of famous steeds. Fans had
the names of their favorites inscribed on walls, lamps, and
pavements. During an excavation archaeologists found a two-
thousand-year-old tribute to a racehorse named Polydoxus
neatly spelled out in mosaic tiles on the floor of a Roman bath:
Vincas, non vincas, te amamus Polydox ("Whether you win or
lose, we love you, Polydoxus!").[4]

Roman interest in racing grew until it became a passion.
By A.D. 500 the three most important buildings in Constantinople, capital of the eastern part of the Roman Empire, were the
emperor's palace, the great church of Holy Wisdom, and the
racetrack (known as the hippodrome).

In Constantinople almost everyone went to the races regularly, and official business was frequently conducted at the
track. From his elaborate box high up in the stands the emperor made speeches on important issues, and rowdy spectators

greeted his ideas with cheers or catcalls. In between races members of the audience discussed politics. The city's two most important political parties, the Blues and Greens, were named after the colored tunics worn by charioteers, and most racegoers belonged to one of these rival bands.

At first the two factions were nothing more than groups of fans who rooted for the charioteer dressed in their favorite color. Later they argued about everything from racing to religious beliefs. But on January 11, 532, in the middle of a race meeting, these two groups joined forces and started to riot against the emperor Justinian's tax policies. From the racetrack the violence spread to every part of the city. Officials were massacred, buildings were burned, and the frightened emperor was ready to flee when government troops finally quelled the uprising.

By the time the great riot broke out at the hippodrome, the ancient golden age of racing was almost at an end. In Rome and Constantinople converts to the new Christian religion were campaigning against the sport on the grounds that it encouraged gambling, cheating, and the worship of idols. In the third century A.D. a stern Christian moralist named Tertullian told his followers that going to the races was just the same as praying to pagan gods. Others agreed, and in 393 the Roman emperor Theodosius I banned all pagan religious festivals—including the ancient Olympic Games.

While moralists condemned the sport, soldiers helped destroy it. In the fourth and fifth centuries A.D., Huns, Vandals, Goths, and other barbarian tribes from the outskirts of the Roman Empire stormed across Europe destroying cities, schools, libraries, and stadiums as they went. Earthquakes rumbled through Constantinople, and in 1204 and 1453 armies sacked the ancient capital. Survivors of these great disasters had little time or money to spend on sport. While they tried to rebuild homes and farms, grass grew over the crumbling ruins of ancient hippodromes, and chariot racing gradually became a forgotten art.

For almost one thousand years racing ceased to be a highly professional, popular public sport—but it didn't disappear entirely. For the next ten centuries it was—for the most part—a private game for wealthy noblemen who owned their own saddle horses.

Organized racing finally started to come back into fashion in 1660, the year Charles II was crowned king of England. Tall, dark, gallant, and witty, this new monarch was a fun-loving gentleman who liked fine dogs, beautiful women, and fast horses. He rode constantly, and when he wasn't attending to official business, Charles arranged race meetings. He encouraged courtiers to ride and gave prizes to the winners. Early in the morning the king was often out watching his horses train. In the afternoons he sometimes rode in races, and in the evenings he occasionally dined with jockeys. Charles's enthusiasm was infectious, and by the end of his reign, flat racing—races in which saddle horses run around an oval dirt or grass track— was well on its way to becoming one of England's favorite sports. For the first time in centuries, new racetracks were built, and large crowds of spectators swarmed into the stands.

Anyone could watch the races, but only a few could actually take part. Wealthy men owned the horses, arranged the contests, and often rode their own animals on the track. A commoner could serve as a nobleman's jockey, but in some places laws prevented working-class men from organizing meets, and those who broke the rules could be severely punished. In 1674 James Bullocke, a Virginia tailor, was fined one hundred pounds of "tobacco and caske" for entering a mare in a race.

The last Horse Race
Run before
CHARLES the Second of
Blessed Memory
By Dorsett Ferry
near
Windsor Castle

King Charles II watches a meet near Windsor Castle shortly before his death in 1685.

While the unhappy tailor fumed, magistrates explained that it was against the law "for a Labourer to make a race" because racing was a "sport only for gentlemen."[5]

And gentlemen certainly liked it. By the eighteenth century the sport was so popular that George Stubbs, a well-known English artist, was able to make a living by painting portraits of the most famous racehorses of his day. Wealthy English owners searched the world for the finest, fastest horses. Three of the animals they brought to England between 1689 and 1728 were destined to make sports history. These horses,

OVERLEAF: "Molly Longlegs," a portrait by George Stubbs

Darley Arabian, Byerley Turk, and Godolphin Arabian, became the ancestors of the world's greatest modern racehorse, the Thoroughbred.

Racing was popular, but not with everyone. Puritans—who also disapproved of card playing and dancing—thought the sport was sinful, and in the seventeenth century they tried to stamp it out in England and the British colonies. During the 1630s straitlaced Puritan elders in Massachusetts sentenced "evill and disordered" colonists who rode and watched horse races to sit in the stocks. But many Americans liked this sinful sport, and by the 1700s there was a public racetrack just across the Massachusetts border in neighboring Rhode Island. During colonial times New Yorkers went to the races. Virginians like George Washington and Thomas Jefferson raced their own horses. And by 1793 there were so many races in Lexington, Kentucky, that crossing the city streets on foot was a risky business.

All over the world interest in racing began to rise. In 1810 Australians cheered their favorites at the first organized race meeting in Sydney. In France Napoleon stopped fighting battles long enough to encourage racing and offer prizes for horse breeding. By 1868 there were race meetings in Rome, and in 1895 fans saw English Thoroughbreds sprint down a Japanese racecourse for the first time.

Today racehorses compete in fifty different countries, and fans watch long races, short races, pony races, endurance races, harness races (in which a trotting horse pulls a light two-wheeled cart called a sulky), and even steeplechases (races in which horses leap over fences placed on the track). The days when racing was a private game for wealthy noblemen have gone forever. In our time anyone can enter a qualified horse in a race, and both men and women now compete on the track.

A bride race in central Asia during the nineteenth century. The woman was supposed to marry the man who caught her, but she could attempt to control the outcome by slowing down, speeding up, changing direction, or striking unwanted suitors with a whip.

For almost three thousand years rules and customs had prevented women from becoming charioteers, jockeys, or racehorse trainers, but in the middle of the twentieth century many of these ancient barriers began to crumble. After a twenty-year legal battle Mrs. Florence Nagel finally won the right to hold a British trainer's license in 1966. Three years later an American, Barbara Jo Rubin, became the first woman jockey to win a race. And in 1972 the powerful Jockey Club, which controls all racing in Britain, finally allowed female jockeys to compete in flat races.

In its long history racing has left its mark on everything

from prayers to politics. In museums admiring visitors stare at portraits of jockeys and horses created by the world's most famous artists. There are plays, movies, songs, and even television shows about racing. Millions who've never set foot on a track have read about horse racing in books, and many television newscasters use racing terms like "photo finish" and "won by a nose" to describe election results. In A.D. 400 residents of the little European country of Estonia used horse races instead of wills to decide who should inherit the family fortune, and in parts of central Asia a suitor still has to win a race to win a bride.

Racing has been called the sport of kings—and the king of sports. Millions have enjoyed it, some have loved it, and a few, like President Andrew Jackson (1767–1845), thought it was an incomparable challenge.

During his long life Jackson was a racehorse owner, an enthusiastic fan, and a fierce, determined competitor. When the president wanted something, he usually got it. And Jackson wanted to own a horse that could beat Captain Jesse Haynie's fast little mare, Maria. But on five separate occasions, in five separate races, Maria trounced Jackson's best blue-ribbon runners. Finally Jackson had to admit defeat, but the memory of the incident rankled.

Many years later, when the former president was a very old man, a friend said, "Tell me, Mr. Jackson, sir, have you ever failed to get something you truly desired?"

For a moment Jackson hesitated. Then the man who'd made a fortune, become a military hero, served in Congress, and been chief executive of the United States replied, "Nothing that I remember—except Haynie's Maria. I never could defeat her."[6]

9. The Wonder-Worker

The year was 1524. General Hernando Cortez, the famed Spanish conqueror of Mexico, was leading a troop of soldiers through Guatemala when his war-horse, Morzillo, suddenly started to limp. Examination showed a long, sharp splinter had pierced the animal's foot. Healing would take days, and the general was in a hurry. Since he couldn't wait for the horse to recover, Cortez asked residents of the nearby town of Tayascal to look after Morzillo until he returned.

The startled Indians agreed to do their best, but they really didn't know where to begin. None of them had ever seen a horse before, and the big black four-legged thing looked dangerous. Finally they decided to treat Morzillo like a king.

Servants kept the horse's manger full of fresh flowers, succulent fruit, and roast fowl. But this rich, exotic diet only made Morzillo sicker, and one dreadful day the poor horse died.

The distraught Indians couldn't replace the stallion, so they decided to give Cortez a statue of his horse instead. The finished sculpture was placed in a temple for safekeeping, and the Indians waited for the general to return.

He never did, and the statue of Morzillo never left the temple. As the years passed, old men showed it to their children and their grandchildren. Storytellers told fabulous tales about this amazing four-legged animal, and soon legends about Morzillo's magic powers began to circulate through the neighborhood.

One hundred years after Cortez's visit, two Catholic friars made their way to Tayascal. They walked into the town's largest temple and stared. There in front of them was a statue of a horse sitting on its haunches. Offerings of fruit and flowers surrounded the image and Indians prayed to it, calling it Tziminchac, lord of thunder. In one short century Morzillo, the lame Spanish war-horse, had become a god.

These events actually took place in a little sixteenth-century Guatemalan town, but they could just as easily have occurred in Europe, Asia, or North Africa before the beginning of the modern scientific era. In those bygone centuries many men and women truly believed that horses could be gods, magicians, and miracle workers. Stories about horses with strange supernatural powers were told in almost every country, and it's easy to understand why. To people who lived before the machine age, a real horse seemed like a fairy-tale creature. It was swift, strong, and beautiful, and it had the power to whisk a traveler to the ends of the earth, bring a warrior victory, feed a family, or help a poor worker make a fortune. To these basic facts, storytellers added a touch of imagination. Then, from this new mixture of fact and fantasy, they wove fabulous tales about magical horses that performed miracles, changed the lives of individuals, and controlled the forces of nature.

Nothing on earth moves faster than time, water, and weather, and the ancients imagined that swift, wonder-working horses helped regulate all three. In those early days many people thought galloping horses carried the life-giving sun across the sky in the daytime, and some believed magical steeds pulled the moon through the heavens at night. Twenty-seven hundred years ago Greeks claimed that Poseidon, the sea god who often appeared in the form of a horse, created the earth's fresh-flowing rivers and streams. Across the world in ancient India men

An eighteenth-century Indian painting of Surya, the Hindu sun god,
driving his chariot across the sky

and women pointed at the scudding rain clouds and said that fierce storm spirits called the Maruts were driving their horse-drawn chariots across the sky. In more recent times Czechs sang about a white horse that brought the winter's snow, and storytellers from certain parts of Russia and central Asia claimed the calendar itself ran on horsepower. Up in the sky, they said, lived a certain magic horse. Year in and year out, he paced around the North Star, pulling the wheel of the seasons, changing summer to autumn and winter to spring.

Sun steeds and storm steeds helped make the land fertile, and so did other horses. Long before the horse became a regular farmhand, men and women apparently thought this strong, energetic animal possessed a life-giving force that made plants grow and animals flourish. The belief was widespread, and people expressed it in different ways. In one part of ancient Greece worshippers prayed before a statue of the harvest goddess, Demeter, that had a woman's body and a horse's head. Old Chinese and Japanese myths say that the first silkworms hatched out of the hide of a dead stallion. Until the nineteenth century farmers in parts of England, France, and Germany thought the corn spirit, a genie that made plants grow, traveled from field

A Japanese votive offering (ema) made about 1840. In ancient times the Japanese offered live horses to the gods. Later they simply donated painted wooden plaques called ema (which means "horse picture") to temples.

to field in the form of a mare. And by about 700–600 B.C. Romans were using horse magic to grow crops.

In those early centuries Rome wasn't the hub of a mighty empire. It was a sleepy little market town nestled among seven green hills on the banks of the Tiber River. Most of its citizens were farmers, and each year on October 15 they left their fields to attend the season's most important agricultural rite, a chariot race.

The race, which was held on the king's fields outside the city, was a fairly ordinary contest, but there was nothing ordinary about the prize. At the finish a priest stabbed one of the victorious chariot horses with a spear, sacrificing it to Mars, the god of war and harvests. Blood from the unlucky victim's body was carefully siphoned into a bottle and later used to purify livestock so the herds would thrive. The horse's tail was carried to the king's house so it could bring health and prosperity to the ruler and the nation. Finally the animal's head was cut off, nailed to a wall, and decorated with a string of loaves so that it would bring Roman farmers a bountiful harvest.[1]

Historians say that humans tamed the horse, but legends say horses helped tame humans. According to the myths, horselike gods and godlike horses provided people with many of the basic elements of civilization. Back at the beginning of time, Chinese storytellers said, a dragon-headed horse brought the legendary emperor Fu-Hsi eight mystic symbols, eight magic keys to the secrets of philosophy, religion, and prophecy. Ancient Greeks told their children about Chiron the Centaur, a wise creature, half man and half horse, who educated the mightiest heroes and taught medicine to the god of healing. Indian mythmakers said that the god Vishnu preserved religious knowledge by donning a horse's head and rescuing the sacred Hindu scriptures from a pair of demons. Romans even claimed

The winged animal on this North African coin minted around 260 B.C. may be Pegasus.

that literature owed a lot to Pegasus, a flying horse, who was said to have created the Hippocrene, a sacred fountain that inspired poets to write great verse.

In addition to giving horses credit for providing the human race with everything from artistic inspiration to medical knowledge, storytellers claimed that some wonder-working horses changed history. In Italy the ancients believed that two magic white steeds, ridden by the demigods Castor and Pollux, swooped down from heaven and helped a hard-pressed Roman army win the battle of Lake Regillus in 496 B.C.

Sensible historians may think architects and engineers helped Emperor Ch'in Shih Huang Ti choose the site of the Great Wall of China, but legends say a wonder-working white horse led construction crews across northern Asia and marked the perfect building location with its hoofprints. Czechs once thought a magic horse chose one of their greatest medieval kings. And in the Near East devout Moslems say that no one paid attention to the words of the religious leader Muhammad (A.D. 570–632) until a winged horse named al-Borak took the unsuccessful prophet on a round-trip ride to heaven for a midnight conference with God.

All these legendary horses were powerful, and all were white. The gods sometimes confided in white horses, heroes rode them, and storytellers often described their magical feats.

But not all horse magicians were white. Until recently men and women in certain parts of rural England believed that a piebald horse could grant a wish if a person walked up to it and said:

> Black's white and white's black
> Over the nag's back.
> Make my wish come true, wish come true
> Wish come very very true.[2]

Eastern European storytellers described another powerful group of horse magicians. In olden times Russian families often huddled around the stove on snowy nights and listened to a tale that began with these words: "Once upon a time, a very long time ago, there lived a poor young peasant named Ivan. He had no money and no land. But he did have one precious possession: a little hunchback horse with magic powers." Then the narrator explained how the little horse carried Ivan to the ends of the earth, saved him from the clutches of an evil king, arranged for him to marry a beautiful princess, and finally helped the young man to win a royal crown.

Today the story of the little hunchback horse is famous, but it is not unique. Dozens of other folktales also chronicle the adventures of old, sick, lame, or misshapen horses that use magic powers to help human heroes win fame and fortune.

All these stories have been told in eastern Europe for centuries, but no one knew why until archaeologists made an extraordinary discovery. While excavating a thousand-year-old cemetery in the Hungarian town of Keszthely, investigators uncovered the remains of crippled, malformed horses in elaborate graves. At first the researchers couldn't imagine why the ancients had buried useless, unattractive animals with such care. Then they noticed that most of the dead horses had an extra tooth or showed signs of lameness, two traits that characterize most of the misshapen horse magicians in folktales. From that piece of information, scholars reasoned that people who lived in eastern Europe around A.D. 500–900 probably believed that flesh-and-blood horses with malformed bodies possessed some sort of supernatural power. During their lives these animals may have received special attention, and after death they were buried with special honors. Stories about the feats these strange horses performed must have been passed on from gen-

This sixteenth-century manuscript illustration shows the prophet
Muhammad *(center)* riding to heaven on al-Borak.

eration to generation, and from those old stories and that ancient belief came fantastic tales that are still told today.

Not every horse was a great magician, but people once believed that almost every part of every horse possessed some sort of magic power. "Fortune," the Arabs said, "is attached to the horse's mane."[3] Eleventh-century Hungarians disagreed. They thought the whole horse's head was a lucky charm and decked their house beams with horse skulls to ensure health, wealth, and happiness.[4] In ancient China doctors prescribed a dose of powdered horse heart for patients who suffered from forgetfulness. Spaniards once thought an amulet made from a piece of stag horn and hair from a black mare's tail could protect a man from evil. The Huns drank horse blood to ratify an oath. Most people thought it was lucky to dream of a horse. And in countries from England to India the horseshoe—which was shaped like the magical moon, made from a magic metal, iron, and worn by a lucky animal—became a token of good fortune.

But as the centuries passed, ideas changed. In most parts of the world people gradually stopped believing in myths and magic. They looked at the heavens through telescopes and saw that horses didn't carry the sun across the sky. They began to study botany and soon discovered that horse magic didn't make crops grow. Slowly the old stories and superstitions were replaced by scientific facts, and by the nineteenth century most Americans and Europeans didn't think any horse could work miracles.

But a scientist proved they were wrong. It happened in the late 1800s, at a time when terrible diphtheria epidemics frequently swept across Europe and America. Each year thousands of children caught the disease, and each year half these young patients died. No one knew how to treat the illness until Dr. Emil Behring found that a chemical—an antitoxin—taken from the blood of an animal infected with diphtheria could cure or immunize a human.

Other scientists soon found that horses could produce enormous quantities of Behring's magic serum, and by the 1920s large herds were helping drug companies provide enough antitoxin to immunize children all over the world. The disease that had killed thousands in the nineteenth century ceased to be a serious threat, and in 1979 there were only sixty-five cases of diphtheria in the entire United States. And this is not a myth, a legend, or a fairy tale. In the modern world, real flesh-and-blood horses performed a real, honest-to-goodness miracle.

10. The Friend

One day about six thousand years ago, somewhere on the vast Eurasian plains, a little wild horse conquered its fear and stood still while a man slipped a halter over its head. It was the first time a human had ever tried to tame a horse. It was also the beginning of a great partnership.

For the next sixty centuries humans and horses worked together, played together, traveled together, and fought together. For almost sixty centuries horses helped rule the world. But the reign of the horse has ended.

Trucks, tractors, and automobiles have replaced horses on farms and highways. Factories no longer run on animal power. Wars are fought with missiles, and the Pony Express is only a memory. Twentieth-century men and women don't need horses, and for the first time in recent history the future of the horse family seems uncertain.

Since 1900 the number of horses in the world has diminished. For thousands of years huge herds of wild horses roamed the great Eurasian plains, but at this moment they are almost extinct. The young ones were caught and tamed, the older ones were slaughtered for food and sport, and slowly the population shrank. By the mid-twentieth century several hundred of these little creatures—called Przewalski's (PSHUH-VAHL-SKEEZ) horses—were living in zoos, but only one small herd remained on the central Asian plains. For many years these animals

Bronze statuette of a Przewalski's horse from Mongolia, made between the fifth and third centuries B.C.

regularly grazed near Takhin Shar-nuru, the Mountain of Yellow Horses, in Mongolia. But in 1977 the herd didn't visit its usual pasture, and it has not been seen since. Perhaps these little horses still live in some hidden valley deep in the central Asian wastelands, but it's not likely. All the available evidence shows that the last true wild horses to live in freedom on the open range have probably perished.

They are not the only victims. In the Australian outback, brumbies—the wild descendants of domestic horses—are considered vermin and shot on sight. Half a world away, in twentieth-century North America, many mustangs have shared the same fate. A century ago some two million of these wild horses roamed the western plains. Settlers and Indians tamed thou-

ONCE UPON A HORSE

sands, and as cattle horses, war-horses, buffalo horses, and workhorses, they helped build the West. In the twentieth century, however, American ranchers don't tame mustangs. They shoot them because wild horses eat up grass intended for sheep and cattle. By 1971 so many mustangs had been killed that Congress passed a law to keep them from being hunted to extinction. Thanks to that legislation, some wild horses still race through the back country in many western states, but the herds are smaller now. In 1983 government officials estimated there were only forty-five thousand mustangs left.

Many domestic horses have already shared the fate of their wild cousins. As the need for horses has diminished, the number of horses owned and used by humans has also declined. Between 1910 and 1920, there were approximately 110 million draft horses and saddle horses in the world. By 1976 that number had fallen to 64 million—a drop of 58 percent. If this downward slide were to continue, the horse would soon be as extinct as the dodo and the dinosaur.

These statistics are depressing, but they don't tell the whole story. There are other facts, and there is a brighter side to the picture.

Today people no longer breed as many horses as they once did. They no longer rely on the horse's strength or depend on its speed. But they still value the horse because this creature possesses another extraordinary talent: the ability to make friends.

Out of the million or so different kinds of animals that inhabit this planet, only two—the horse and the dog—consistently return affection, display loyalty, and show gratitude for good care. For six thousand years horses have given humans their love, and men and women have returned the favor.

In 326 B.C. Alexander the Great named a city after his be-

OVERLEAF: Frederick George Cotman painted "One of the Family" during the nineteenth century, when humans and horses still worked and lived side by side.

loved horse, Bucephalus. Ancient Persians showed their respect by adding the word *aspa* (which means "horse") to the names of gods and heroes. During the American Revolution colonial patriot Samuel Dexter established a retirement fund for his horse. In England the Duke of Wellington (1769–1852) buried his charger with full military honors. And out on the Great Plains of nineteenth-century North America Blackfeet warriors, trained to bear hunger, pain, and thirst without complaint, wept openly when their horses died.

Generations of artists praised the horse's grace and beauty. Storytellers described its faithfulness and courage. Some men and women once worshipped this animal. Today people are showing their affection for the horse in a different way: they are helping to ensure its survival.

The U.S. government's Bureau of Land Management has found a way to save horses. Instead of shooting mustangs to keep the herds down to a reasonable size, they periodically round up a number of these wild horses and put them up for adoption.

Scientists have been busy, too. At an international conference held in Moscow in 1985, zoologists started making plans to bring true wild horses back to the wild. Curators at major European and American zoos have begun breeding a special group of Przewalski's horses, able to survive the hardships of living in the wilderness. If everything goes according to schedule, the first of these zoo-bred animals will be released in the 1990s, and once again true wild horses will gallop across the windswept plains of their ancient homelands.

Domestic horses also have friends, and in recent years people have started to discover and rediscover all the jobs that horses can do.

In 1980 the U.S. Border Patrol turned back the clock.

RIGHT: This early twentieth-century poster is a poignant reminder of the long friendship between horses and humans.

They started to use riders to police the U.S.-Mexico frontier because experiments showed horses could traverse this stretch of rough country better than squad cars.

In the past few years teachers have discovered that riding helps retarded children develop balance and physical coordination. Reform school officials at the Borstal and Detention Centre in Hollesley, England, believe that working with horses improves the behavior of teenage lawbreakers at their institution. Doctors often prescribe riding for disabled patients who need physical exercise, and police chiefs have started to put horses back on the duty roster. Since research has shown that officers can control crowds and patrol neighborhoods more efficiently on horseback than in cars or on foot, mounted police have been returning to the streets of European and American cities.

Out in the country some horses are now plowing fields and harvesting crops just as their ancestors did. In Pennsylvania and parts of the Midwest the Amish people, famed for their farming skills, use horses to cultivate their land. Farmers in many less-developed countries still depend on animal power, and agricultural experts in highly industrialized countries have started to take a new look at one of the world's oldest farmhands. Some modern farmers have become interested in using horses because they think tractors damage the soil by packing it down too solidly. Oil shortages and the high cost of fuel inspired others to substitute animals for machines. England's Agricultural Training Board started a class for people interested in learning to use horses on farms, and in the 1970s the demand for Shires, Suffolks, and other huge workhorses actually increased.

Most farmers still aren't ready to trade their tractors for horses, but that could change. Scientists have repeatedly warned that the world's oil supply is limited. No one knows how

RIGHT: Pee Wee, a miniature horse ridden by young Heather Roberts, and Time Piece, a full-sized show horse ridden by Cathy Dress

much is left, but if the wells run dry before researchers discover another energy source, farmers and everyone else may have to depend on the old-fashioned muscle power of the horse.

Future generations may or may not need horses for work, but they probably will use horses for fun. In circuses and rodeos, on racetracks and riding trails, in show rings and films, horses now entertain millions. Interest in equestrian sports seems to be on the rise, and that's good news. Since 1960 the number of professional racehorses has increased. The number of racehorse breeders has increased. And, best of all, the U.S. horse population has increased because so many people have purchased their own pleasure horses.

Athletes and audiences have done a great deal to ensure the horse's survival, but so have stockmen. Because most modern families don't have the money or the space to support a full-size horse, breeders have recently developed a line of miniature mares and stallions. These tiny animals, known as Falabella horses, stand about thirty inches tall, weigh about ninety pounds, and are small enough to live inside a house. One day Falabellas may become popular pets. If they do, there's a chance the horse family will end as it began—with a tiny creature no bigger than a dog.

The long story of the partnership between horses and humans isn't over yet. A large part of the chronicle remains to be written. In the next six thousand years will the horse be a worker, a pet, an entertainer, a friend, or simply a memory? No one knows what future chapters will say, but long ago Moslem storytellers made a prediction. Back at the very beginning of time, they said, God called to the Wind. "Mother of Tempests," He cried, "I command you to bring forth a creature that will fly without wings, fight against my enemies, and faithfully serve all those who follow my laws." The Wind obeyed, and in a little while she gave birth to the most beautiful of all living creatures: the horse.

As soon as it could, the little newborn foal stood up on its long, wobbly legs. It bowed before the Ruler of the Universe, and God smiled. "Little horse," He said, "rejoice, for you are the most blessed of all creatures. In days to come you will travel all over the earth. Happiness will always be yours, and the people of all nations will love and cherish you."

Notes

1. The Dawn Horse

1. Investigators think early hunters killed these animals by driving herds over the edge of a cliff adjacent to the site.

2. The Servant

1. Jankovich, *They Rode Through Europe,* 42. Many letters from Kassite princes end this way. The Kassites were an ancient horse-owning people who originally lived in what is now Iran, near the border of southern Russia. At some time between 1800 and 1500 B.C., they conquered parts of Mesopotamia, and they may well have been the people who taught Mesopotamians how to use horses.
2. For horses the trip to the New World wasn't easy. During the voyage fickle winds often left sailing ships becalmed for days in the calms of Cancer at 30° N. latitude and the calms of Capricorn at 30° S. latitude. In these hot climates the ships' drinking-water supplies were quickly exhausted, and after a few days the horses on the motion-less ships began to go mad with thirst. Sailors shot the wretched creatures and threw their bodies to the sharks, giving the regions a name they still bear: the Horse Latitudes.
3. Ernst August, Elector of Hanover (1629–1698), quoted in Cohen, J. M., and M. J. Cohen, eds., *The Penguin Dictionary of Quotations* (Harmondsworth, England: Penguin, 1972), 181.
4. Both large and small breeds lived in Eurasia during the Ice Age. Investigations have shown that between about 3000 and 1000 B.C. the size of European horses ranged from eleven to fifteen hands (one hand is equal to four inches). Today wild horses (also known as Przewalski's horses) are about twelve to fourteen hands high. The largest living domestic horses are eighteen hands, and the word "pony" is used to describe certain animals that measure less than 14.2 hands. Mustangs, the wild descendants of domestic horses, are usually somewhat smaller than their tame ancestors. They are, it seems, living proof that good care and careful breeding have helped increased the horse's size over the centuries.

3. The War-Horse

1. Silverberg, *The Great Wall of China,* 136. The author of this passage, thirteenth-century historian Matthew of Paris, was not exaggerating. Scholars estimate that between 1211 and 1223 Genghis Khan and his men slaughtered approximately 18.5 million people.

2. The size of a knight's horse was, to some extent, determined by the weight of his armor. Before 1300 knights wore fairly lightweight suits of flexible chain mail, and a medium-sized horse could easily carry a knight (a 140-pound man plus about 60 pounds of armor, weapons, and trappings) into battle. Unfortunately, arrows could pierce chain mail, so in the fourteenth century craftsmen started to make arrow-proof armor out of metal plates. The new suits were much heavier, and experts figure the total weight of a man, plate armor, weapons, and trappings would have been about 405 pounds. To bear this enormous load, huge horses were developed by breeders. Those over-size war-horses were probably the ancestors of many large modern workhorses, like the Shire.

3. The rest of this passage can be found in the Bible's Book of Revelation, Chapter 6. The horses ridden by these terrible apparitions are pale, red, black, and white. Death rides the pale horse; War, the red one; Famine, the black; and Conquest, the white.

4. Cavalrymen broke an infantry square on only one occasion. In 1812, at García Hernandez, Spain, a British horseman and his mount were killed during an attack on French infantry. Although dead, the horse kept moving and did something it would never have done alive: It plunged into the French ranks and opened up a path for the rest of the British cavalry.

5. Ellis, *Cavalry: The History of Mounted Warfare,* 182. After the 1930s horses went into battle on very few occasions. During World War II Russian cavalrymen on tough little Siberian ponies successfully attacked German tanks immobilized by subzero winter temperatures. In Kenya during the 1950s, mounted soldiers attacked Mau Mau rebels, and a mare named Reckless was awarded the rank of sergeant in the U.S. Army for hauling ammunition to American marines during the Korean War. Her story has been told in Andrew Geer's *Reckless: Pride of the Marines* (New York: Dutton, 1950).

4. The Traveler

1. Scholars have calculated that the price of a horse in ancient Greece was ten to eighty times the price of an ox.

2. The ancients realized that this inefficient type of harness prevented horses from drawing heavy loads, and in A.D. 438 the Roman emperor Theodosius II passed a law stating that a team of horses could not pull a loaded vehicle weighing more than 1,100 pounds.

3. Some think that the first sidesaddle was actually a pack saddle equipped with a plank that served as a footrest. This device, which may have originated in central Asia, first became popular in southern Europe in the twelfth century and was used in England by about 1380.

4. Paul Angle, ed., *A Lincoln Reader* (New Brunswick, N.J.: Rutgers University Press, 1947), 99. Canvassing was a tough, dangerous job for both men and horses. During the

1840 presidential campaign one of candidate William Henry Harrison's supporters traveled almost a thousand miles in a single month. Another had his speechmaking trip interrupted when ruffians pushed a large rock over the edge of a cliff in order to block the passage of his carriage.

5. Dobie, *The Mustangs,* 21. Some early explorers owed their lives to horses. When sixteenth-century Spanish traveler Gonzalo Silvestre was lost in a swamp, his intelligent mount sniffed out a trail and carried him to safety.

6. Dunlop, *Wheels West 1590–1900,* 152.

7. Carson, *Men, Beasts and Gods,* 90. Horses apparently knew who their friends were. According to one old story, when working conditions became unbearable, the streetcar horses on New York's Fourth Avenue line would stop in front of the ASPCA building and wait stubbornly until one of the society's humane officers came out to alleviate their suffering.

5. THE MESSENGER

1. Howard *et al., Hoofbeats of Destiny,* 150. At the outset owners of the Pony Express tried to buy horses that were "well broke to saddle." Later, however, the chronic need for replacements forced them to purchase untrained mustangs and Indian ponies. Stationmasters, who supposedly had a lot of free time, were in charge of breaking the animals, but training was usually rather haphazard.

6. THE WORKHORSE

1. Nailed horseshoes were not commonly used in Europe until the ninth century A.D., though they may have been invented by the Celts around A.D. 100.

2. Nineteenth-century American cowboys weren't the first to herd cattle on horseback. Nomads who traveled by horse probably invented the system in ancient times. In medieval Spain mounted cowboys also herded cattle; and later, in the New World, Spanish colonists used these old herding techniques on Mexican and South American ranches. Seventeenth-century English settlers organized the first cattle drives in North America, and in 1655 Puritan cowboys took a herd from Springfield, Massachusetts, to the Boston Common.

3. The term *horsepower* was actually coined by James Watt, inventor of the steam engine. In the eighteenth century there was no accurate way to describe the amount of work a machine could do, so Watt invented a new unit of measurement. He calculated that a single workhorse could lift 33,000 pounds a distance of one foot in one minute. Since a machine that could do this amount of work was as strong as one horse, Watt dubbed it a "one horsepower" engine.

7. THE GAME PLAYER

1. Broderick, *Animals in Archaeology,* 75. Amenhotep III was an energetic hunter and a boastful one. Today we know a great deal about his favorite sport because Amenhotep ordered scribes to write descriptions of his expeditions and had craftsmen record the number of animals he killed on scarabs that were given to royal courtiers.

2. Ellis, *Cavalry: The History of Mounted Warfare,* 116. Strangely enough, the sport that helped produce so many fine Mongol warriors also killed the Mongols' greatest leader. In 1227 Genghis Khan, one of the finest cavalry generals in history, died after being thrown from his horse during a hunt.

3. Jonathan D. Spence, *Emperor of China: Self-Portrait of K'ang-hsi* (New York: Vintage Books, 1975), 12. K'ang-hsi, who was a descendant of the Manchu (a tribe of nomadic horsemen that conquered China in the seventeenth century), understood and loved horses. He ordered shamans to pray for his steeds. He thought that good mounted archers had to start their training as children, and he firmly believed that a horse could bring out the best qualities in a man and a man the best qualities in a horse.

4. Jankovich, *They Rode Through Europe,* 144. Nur ad-Din may have been the most famous general to use polo as a military exercise, but he wasn't the only one. In Japan a type of polo called *dakyu* was a standard part of an eighteenth-century knight's training program.

5. Oakshott, *A Knight and His Horse,* 32. Depriving a tournament contestant of his prize was a very serious punishment. Although most knights fought for fun or exercise, there were a few professional jousters who lived on their prizes. At tournaments two kinds of prizes were usually given: a prize offered by a tournament host, and the right to hold a defeated knight for ransom. Rules stated that the loser of a contest had to give the winner his horse and armor or an equivalent sum of money. Since armor and horses were valuable, a good professional jouster could make a handsome profit in a single afternoon.

6. Ellis, *Cavalry: The History of Mounted Warfare,* 17.

7. Chenevix-Trench, *A History of Horsemanship,* 103. One of the first eighteenth-century commanders to agree with Blunderville was the German ruler Frederick the Great (1740–1786). Frederick was more impressed by a cavalryman who could gallop between the turning arms of a windmill (as one of his generals did) than by haut école tricks. When he found out that his academy-trained cavalrymen were so interested in maintaining perfect form that they moved slowly and avoided rough terrain, he ordered his generals to teach them cross-country riding techniques instead.

8. THE RACEHORSE

1. Seth-Smith, *The Horse in Art and History,* 24. Some Greek racehorses were so well trained that they needed little help from riders and drivers. Ancient sources report that when the jockey riding a mare that belonged to Pheidolas of Corinth fell off at the beginning of a race, his horse galloped on alone. She dodged past all the other horses, completed the required number of laps, and then stopped in front of the judges to receive her prize.

2. Vesey-Fitzgerald, *The Book of the Horse,* 77. Cynisca was the first princess to take part in the Olympic Games, but certainly not the last. In 1976 Britain's Princess Anne joined her country's team and competed in the Three Day Event (a test that includes dressage, cross-country riding, and jumping) at the Montreal Olympics.

3. The emperor Nero (A.D. 37–68) actually tried to drive a ten-horse chariot in the Olympic Games. During the race this fat, inept Roman fell out of his chariot, was helped

back in, and then quit before finishing the course. Cowardly judges gave the emperor a prize for this disgusting performance, and Nero celebrated his "triumph" for weeks afterward.

4. Carcopino, *Daily Life in Ancient Rome,* 219.

5. Stanard, "Racing in Colonial Virginia," 294. Until the last part of the twentieth century racing was so closely associated with the upper classes that during the Russian Revolution (1917–18) Bolshevik rebels tried and executed a racehorse for the crime of associating with the hated nobility.

6. Hunt, *Horses and Heroes: The Story of the Horse in America for 450 Years,* 71. Among the wonderful stories in Hunt's book is the one about Jackson's friend, the Rev. Cryer, who almost lost his job when church officials discovered he was racing "half a horse."

9. THE WONDER-WORKER

1. Long after ancient times people in many parts of the world continued to believe that horses had the power to help crops grow and herds prosper. In the early 1900s Batak tribesmen who lived on the hot, jungly island of Sumatra regularly sacrificed a red horse or sometimes a buffalo to cleanse their fields of evil. In some parts of India villagers still ask the horse-shaped god, Dudhere, to make their cows produce plenty of milk. Travelers in nineteenth-century England occasionally saw the body of a dead horse hanging from a tree because at that time a few British farmers still believed that killing a horse brought good luck to cattle.

2. Tongue, *Somerset Folklore,* 54. In Somerset, England, some people refused to buy white-legged horses because of an old rhyme that went:

> Three white feet don't try it or buy it,
> If it's a present don't ride it yourself;
> Wrap it up in paper and put it on the shelf.

The Arabs thought that a horse with three white stockings was perfectly all right but that one with four white stockings was a second-rate animal.

3. Hanauer, *Folklore of the Holyland,* 201.

4. People in many other parts of the world also thought the horse's head was a powerful charm. In relatively recent times some Japanese farmers hung horse heads over the farmhouse doors to bring good luck. This concept also turns up in folklore; an old Gypsy legend from eastern Europe tells of a horse's head that saves a man's life and helps him marry a beautiful princess. "The Goose Girl" by Jakob and Wilhelm Grimm relates a similar story.

Principal Sources

An asterisk indicates a book of special interest to young readers.

Aldington, Richard, and Delano Ames, trans. *New Larousse Encyclopedia of Mythology.* London: Hamlyn, 1959.

Anderson, J. K. *Ancient Greek Horsemanship.* Berkeley: University of California Press, 1961.

Azzaroli, A. *An Early History of Horsemanship.* Leiden: E. J. Brill/Dr. W. Backhuys, 1985.

Barclay, Harold B. *The Role of the Horse in Man's Culture.* London: J. A. Allen, 1980.

Blackstone, G. V. *A History of the British Fire Service.* London: Routledge & Kegan Paul, 1957.

*Bloss, Roy S. *Pony Express: The Great Gamble.* Berkeley: Howell-North, 1959.

Bökönyi, S. *History of Domestic Mammals in Central and Eastern Europe.* Translated by Lili Halápy. Budapest: Akadémiai Kiadó, 1974.

Braider, Donald. *The Life, History, and Magic of the Horse.* New York: Grosset & Dunlap, 1973.

Brereton, J. M. *The Horse in War.* Newton Abbott: David & Charles, n.d.

Bright, John. *Pit Ponies.* London: B. T. Batsford, 1986.

Broderick, A. Houghton, ed. *Animals in Archaeology.* New York: Praeger, 1972.

Carcopino, Jérôme. *Daily Life in Ancient Rome.* Edited by Henry T. Rowell and translated by E. O. Lorimer. New Haven: Yale University Press, 1940.

Carson, Gerald. *Men, Beasts and Gods.* New York: Scribner's, 1972.

Chambers, James. *The Devil's Horsemen: The Mongol Invasion of Europe.* New York: Atheneum, 1979.

Chenevix-Trench, Charles. *A History of Horsemanship.* Garden City, N.Y.: Doubleday, 1970.

Clabby, John. *The Natural History of the Horse.* New York: Taplinger, 1976.

Clark, LaVerne Harrell. *They Sang for Horses: The Impact of the Horse on Navajo and Apache Folklore.* Tucson: University of Arizona Press, 1966.

Denhardt, Robert M. *The Horse of the Americas.* Norman: University of Oklahoma Press, 1948.

Denison, George T. *A History of Cavalry from the Earliest Times.* Westport, Conn.: Greenwood Press, 1977.

Dent, Anthony. *The Horse Through Fifty Centuries of Civilization.* New York: Holt, Rinehart & Winston, 1974.

*Dobie, J. Frank. *The Mustangs.* New York: Bramhall House, 1934.

Drower, M. S. "The Domestication of the Horse" in *The Domestication of Plants and Animals,* edited by Peter J. Ucko and G. W. Dimbleby. London: Gerald Duckworth, 1969.

Dunlop, Richard. *Wheels West 1590–1900.* Chicago: Rand McNally, 1977.

Edwards, Elwyn Hartley, ed. *Encyclopedia of the Horse.* London: Octopus Books, 1977.

Ellis, John. *Cavalry: The History of Mounted Warfare.* New York: Putnam, 1978.

Evans, George Ewart. *The Horse in the Furrow.* London: Faber & Faber, 1960.

————. *Horse Power and Magic.* London: Faber & Faber, 1979.

*Fox, Charles Philip. *A Pictorial History of Performing Horses.* Seattle: Superior Publishing Co., 1960.

Frazer, James George. *The Golden Bough.* New York: Macmillan, 1963.

Gunderson, Robert Gray. *The Log Cabin Campaign.* Lexington: University of Kentucky Press, 1957.

Haines, Francis. *Horses in America.* New York: Crowell, 1971.

Hanauer, J. E. *Folklore of the Holyland.* London: Sheldon Press, 1935.

Harlow, Alvin P. *Old Post Bags.* New York: D. Appleton, 1928.

Hawks, Ellison. *The Romance of Transport.* New York: Crowell, n.d.

Hill, Michael. "Pit Ponies Still Plod On." London Sunday *Times,* Oct. 22, 1978: 19.

*Howard, Robert West. *The Horse in America.* Chicago: Follett, 1965.

*————. *The Great Iron Trail: The Story of the First Transcontinental Railroad.* New York: Putnam, 1962.

*————, Roy E. Coy, Frank C. Robertson, and Agnes Wright Spring. *Hoofbeats of Destiny.* New York: New American Library, 1960.

Howey, M. Oldfield. *The Horse in Magic and Myth.* London: William Rider & Son, 1923.

*Hunt, Frazier, and Robert Hunt. *Horses and Heroes: The Story of the Horse in America for 450 Years.* New York: Scribner's, 1949.

Jankovich, Miklós. *They Rode Through Europe.* Translated by Anthony Dent. New York: Scribner's, 1971.

Josephy, Alvin M., ed. *The American Heritage Book of Indians.* American Heritage Publishing Company, 1961.

Keegan, John. *The Face of Battle.* New York: Viking Press, 1976.

Lewinsohn, Richard. *Animals, Men and Myths.* London: Victor Gollancz, 1954.

Mack, Edward C. *Peter Cooper: Citizen of New York.* New York: Duell, Sloan & Pearce, 1949.

Margetson, Stella. *Journey by Stages: Some Account of the People Who Travelled by Stage-Coach and Mail in the Years Between 1660 and 1840.* London: Cassell, 1967.

*Martin, Ann. *Equestrian Woman.* New York: Paddington Press, 1979.

McGovern, William Montgomery. *The Early Empires of Central Asia: A Study of the Scythians and the Huns and the Part They Played in World History.* Chapel Hill: University of North Carolina Press, 1939.

Mora, Jo. *Trail Dust and Saddle Leather.* New York: Scribner's, 1946.

*Oakshott, R. Ewart. *A Knight and His Horse.* London: Lutterworth Press, 1962.

Rees, James. *Footprints of a Letter-Carrier.* Philadelphia: Lippincott, 1866.

Root, Waverley. *Food: An Authoritative and Visual History and Dictionary of the Foods of the World.* New York: Simon & Schuster, 1980.

Sandoz, Mari. *The Cattlemen: From the Rio Grande Across the Far Marias.* New York: Hastings House, 1958.

Schöbel, Heinz. *The Ancient Olympic Games.* Translated by John Becker. Princeton, N.J.: D. Van Nostrand, 1966.

Selby-Lowndes, Joan. *The First Circus: The Story of Philip Astley.* London: Lutterworth, 1957.

Seth-Smith, Michael, ed. *The Horse in Art and History.* New York: Mayflower Books, 1978.

Silverberg, Robert. *The Great Wall of China.* Philadelphia: Chilton Books, 1965.

Simpson, George Gaylord. *Horses: The Story of the Horse Family in the Modern World and Through Sixty Million Years of History.* New York: Oxford University Press, 1951.

Simross, Lynn. "LAPD Experimenting with Mounted Units in Crowd Control." Los Angeles *Times,* April 10, 1981: Pt. 5.

Smollar, Dave. "Returning Wild Horses to the Wild." Los Angeles *Times,* May 5, 1986: Pt. 1, 3 and 18.

Stanard, W. G. "Racing in Colonial Virginia." *Virginia Magazine of History and Biography,* Vol. 2, Oct. 27, 1895, 294ff.

Tongue, R. L. *Somerset Folklore.* Vol. 8, *County Folklore.* London: Folklore Society, 1965.

Turner, E. S. *May It Please Your Lordship.* London: Michael Joseph, 1971.

Van Gulik, R. H. *Hayagriva: The Mantrayanic Aspect of Horse-Cult in China and Japan.* Leiden: E. J. Brill, 1935.

Vaux-Phalipau, M. de. *Les chevaux merveilleux dans l'histoire, la légende, les contes populaires.* Paris: J. Peyronnet, 1939.

Vernam, Glenn R. *Man on Horseback.* New York: Harper & Row, 1964.

Vesey-Fitzgerald, Brian. *The Book of the Horse.* Los Angeles: Broden, 1947.

Vignernon, Paul. *Le cheval dans l'antiquité Greco-Romaine.* Nancy: Faculté des Lettres et des Sciences humaines de l'Université de Nancy, 1968.

Walker, George. *Haste, Post, Haste: Postmen and Post-Roads Through the Ages.* London: Harrap, 1938.

White, Lynn. *Medieval Technology and Social Change.* London: Oxford University Press, 1962.

Wright, Richardson. *Hawkers and Walkers in Early America.* Philadelphia: Lippincott, 1927.

Facing title page: Detail of an Etruscan bronze urn; page 19: Detail of the Royal Standard of Ur; page 34: Relief showing the war against the Arabs from the North. Palace of King Ashurbanipal, Nineveh; page 47; page 58: Warrior on horseback from Grumentum, Lucania, c. 550 B.C.; page 60; page 76: "Oiwake stage with a perspective of Mt. Asama," woodblock print by Keisai Eisen, no. 21 in the series "The Sixty-nine Stations of the Kisokado," c. 1835–42; page 86; page 112; page 130: Black-figure amphora by the Eucharides Painter; page 132; page 137: "The Last Horse Race Run before Charles the Second" engraved by Francis Barlow, 1687; Reproduced by Courtesy of the Trustees of the British Museum. Page 10: Detail from jacket painting by Linda Storm. Page 13: Neg. no. 46616. (Photo by A. E. Anderson); page 14: "Eohippus" by Charles R. Knight. Neg. no. 312630. (Photo by H. S. Rice); Courtesy Department of Library Services, American Museum of Natural History. Page 17: The "Chinese" horse from Lascaux. Courtesy Caisse Nationale des Monuments Historiques et des Sites. © ARS/N.Y./ARCH. PHOT. PARIS/SPADEM 1989. Page 22: Bronze buckle, north central Caucasus, early first millennium B.C., M.76.97.654, the Nasli M. Heeramaneck Collection; page 23: Bronze plaque, Mongolia, 200 B.C.–A.D. 200, M.76.97.582, the Nasli M. Heeramaneck Collection of Near Eastern Art, Gift of the Ahmanson Foundation; page 150: The Miraj or Night Journey of Muhammad Miniature from a Manuscript of a Khamsa of Nizami, Shiraz 924 A.H. (A.D. 1517), M.73.5.421, the Nasli M. Heeramaneck Collection, Gift of Joan Palevsky; page 154: Bronze horse (Equus Przewalskii), Mongolia, 5th–3rd centuries B.C., M.76.97.558c, the Nasli M. Heeramaneck Collection of Near Eastern Art, Gift of the Ahmanson Foundation; The Los Angeles County Museum of Art. Page 24: "Lancer of the Sultan of Begharmi" in Denham, Dixon, Capt. Clapperton and Dr. Oudney. *Narrative of Travels and Discoveries in Northern and Central Africa in the Years 1822, 1823, 1824.* London: J. M. Murray, 1826. Page 27; page 48: Illustration from Froissart's *Chronicles,* copy made for Louis de Bruges c. 1460. Ms. Fr. 2643, f.207; page 118: Illustration from René d'Anjou's *Traité de la Forme et Devis d'un Tournois;* Photographs courtesy of the Bibliothêque Nationale, Paris. Page 28: "Vue de Versailles" by Jean-Baptiste Martin. Musée de Versailles. © Cliché des Musées Nationaux, Paris. Page 33: From Layard, A. H. *Nineveh and Its Remains.* New York: Putnam, 1854. Page 35, page 134: Photos by David Tripp. Courtesy of The Johns Hopkins University. Page 39, page 141: From Knox, Thomas W. *The Travels of Marco Polo for Boys and Girls.* New York: Putnam, 1885. Page 40: E33-1964; page 46: IS125-1954; page 117: E2601-1910; page 145: D379-1889; By courtesy of the Board of Trustees of the Victoria and Albert Museum. Page 43: Illustration from Queen Mary's Psalter, folio 56; page 62: Illustration from the Luttrell Psalter; Courtesy of the British Library. Page 44: Illustration from King René's *Le Cueur d'Amours Espris.* Cod. 2597, folio 21 verso. Courtesy of the Bild-Archiv der Österreichischen

Nationalbibliothek, Vienna. Pages 50–51: Detail from "The Thin Red Line" by Robert Gibb. Courtesy of the Director, National Army Museum London. Page 53: ICHi-06777; page 79: South Water Street, west from Dearborn. ICHi-04710; Chicago Historical Society. Page 54; pages 68–69: "The Life of a Fireman: The Metropolitan System," Currier & Ives, 1866; page 83: "The 'Minute-Men' of the Revolution," Currier & Ives, 1876; pages 122–23: "The Pursuit" after A. F. Tait, Currier & Ives, 1856; Courtesy of the Library of Congress. Page 59: From Layard, A. H. *Nineveh und seine Ueberreste.* Leipzig: Dyk'sche Buchhandlung, 1854. Page 61: From Lacroix, Paul. *Directoire, Consulat et Empire: Moeurs et Usages, Lettres, Sciences et Arts.* Paris: Firmin-Didot, 1884. Fig. 56. Pages 64–65: From Apperly, Charles James [Nimrod]. *The Chace, the Turf, and the Road.* London: John Murray, 1870. Pages 66–67: The Garden Seat Horse Bus. Courtesy of the London Transport Museum. Page 70: "Mounted Policemen Arresting Burglars Uptown in New York" by Frederic Remington. From Jackson, Marta, ed. *The Illustrations of Frederic Remington with a Commentary by Owen Wister.* New York: Bounty Books, 1970. Courtesy of the Crown Publishing Group. Page 73: "Pittsford on the Erie Canal (A Sultry Calm)." Watercolor by George Harvey, c. 1840. New York State Historical Association, Cooperstown. Page 75: "Daniel Boone Escorting Settlers Through the Cumberland Gap" by George Caleb Bingham, 1851–52. Washington University Gallery of Art, St. Louis. Gift of Nathaniel Phillips, Boston, 1890. Page 80: Courtesy of the Union Pacific Railroad. Page 85: Photo by Adolfo Tomeucci in Von Hagen, Victor W. *The Roads That Led to Rome.* London: George Weidenfeld & Nicolson, 1967. Pages 88–89: "All Right" by C. C. Henderson. Photo courtesy of the Post Office. Crown Copyright. Page 91: By permission of the U.S. Secret Service, Department of the Treasury. Page 95: M. 399, folio 10v; page 114: M. 820, folio 12; The Pierpont Morgan Library, New York. Page 97: Photograph courtesy of Oregon State University Archives, P89:394. Page 98: From Lacroix, Paul. *Moeurs, Usages et Costumes au Moyen Age et à l'époque de la Renaissance.* Paris: Firmin-Didot, 1878. Fig. 97. Page 99: Illustration from Agricola, *De Re Metallica,* Book 6, p. 128. Basle, 1561. By permission of the Syndics of Cambridge University Library. Pages 100–101: "Buffalo Chase by a Female" by A. J. Miller. The Walters Art Gallery, Baltimore. Page 104: Illustration by Frederic Remington in Roosevelt, Theodore. *Ranch Life and the Hunting Trail.* New York: The Century, 1888. Page 106: Roundup on the Sherman ranch near Genesse, Kansas. Kansas State Historical Society, Topeka. Page 108: Union Pacific Railroad Museum Collection. Print no. H11-76. Page 109: Courtesy of the British Coal Corporation, Central Records Dept., National Workshops, Tursdale, Co. Durham. Page 120: Pluvinel, Antoine de, rev. by René de Menon. *L'Instruction du Roy en l'Exercise de Monter à Cheval.* Amsterdam: J. Schipper, 1666. Fig. 23. General Research Division; p. 121: Newcastle, William Cavendish. *General System of Horsemanship.* London: J. Brindley, 1743. Vol. I, plate 28 (detail). Print Collection, Miriam and Ira D. Wallach

Index